Chocolate Covered Murder
A Pumpkin Hollow Mystery,
book 3
by
Kathleen Suzette

Books by Kathleen Suzette:

A Rainey Daye Cozy Mystery Series

Chocolate Heart Killer
A Pumpkin Hollow Mystery, book 14
Strawberry Creams and Death
A Pumpkin Hollow Mystery, book 15
Pumpkin Spice Lies
A Pumpkin Hollow Mystery, book 16
A Freshly Baked Cozy Mystery Series
Apple Pie A La Murder,
A Freshly Baked Cozy Mystery, Book 1
Trick or Treat and Murder,
A Freshly Baked Cozy Mystery, Book 2
Thankfully Dead
A Freshly Baked Cozy Mystery, Book 3
Candy Cane Killer
A Freshly Baked Cozy Mystery, Book 4
Ice Cold Murder
A Freshly Baked Cozy Mystery, Book 5
Love is Murder
A Freshly Baked Cozy Mystery, Book 6
Strawberry Surprise Killer
A Freshly Baked Cozy Mystery, Book 7
Plum Dead
A Freshly Baked Cozy Mystery, book 8
Red, White, and Blue Murder
A Freshly Baked Cozy Mystery, book 9
Mummy Pie Murder
A Freshly Baked Cozy Mystery, book 10
A Gracie Williams Mystery Series
Pushing Up Daisies in Arizona,

Table of Contents

Chapter One

"I PROMISE YOU, THERE is no curse on Pumpkin Hollow," I assured the woman standing in front of me. "Sometimes people around here let their imaginations run wild." I was ringing up candy for her at the cash register and trying to do damage control at the same time.

The woman looked at me with suspicion, not quite believing what I was telling her. I gave her a winning smile to try to convince her. A rumor was going around town that Pumpkin Hollow was cursed, and the rumor was spreading to the tourists. It wasn't the first time rumors of the witchy kind went around, and while it would appeal to certain types of tourists, we were a family-oriented Halloween-themed town, and it might put off other potential tourists that had small children.

Pumpkin Hollow is located in the mountains of Northern California, and we celebrate Halloween all year long. But the weeks between Labor Day and two weeks after Halloween were what we called the Halloween season. During that time we saw large numbers of tourists that flocked to the town to see the sights, visit the attractions, and enjoy the beautiful fall weather.

"Well, I've heard there's a curse," the woman said, with finality. She was middle-aged and wore a floppy straw hat with a tiny scarecrow affixed to the front. I vaguely remembered seeing her around town before, but I was pretty sure she wasn't a local.

"Just the locals spreading rumors," I said, waving my hand as if I could wave the rumors away. I smiled even bigger in an attempt to convince her. There wasn't much I could do to change people's minds about certain things, but maybe I could distract them. "Would you be interested in a sample of our cinnamon fudge?" When things get uncomfortable, change the subject and offer candy. It was practically my life's motto.

"Cinnamon fudge?" the woman asked, her eyes lighting up. "I've never tasted cinnamon fudge before. I would love to try some."

"It's the best. My mother makes it fresh every day," I said, trimming off a small sample sized piece with a plastic knife. I placed it in a tiny paper cup and handed it to her.

"Oh my gosh," she said as she rolled the sample around in her mouth and closed her eyes. "This is wonderful!"

"How much would you like today?" I asked. I wasn't being presumptuous. Once tasted, my mother's fudge had to be purchased.

"A quarter of a pound," the woman said, eyeing the different flavors of fudge in the display case. "Oh, and a quarter-pound of the peanut butter fudge, too. I may as well get some while I'm here."

My parents owned the Pumpkin Hollow Candy Store, handed down to them from my mother's parents, and I was now an employee there. It wasn't what I envisioned my life to be, though. After high school, I had moved away to go to college in Michigan, and after ten years in college, I was the proud owner of three master's degrees. When I realized that I might be running away from life by staying in college and changing my degree year after year, I finally returned home. And while I was thrilled to be home, I was a little disappointed that I wasn't putting my education to work. I spent a lot of time trying not to think about the fact that if all I was going to do with my life was work at my parent's candy shop, I could have stayed put after high school and avoided the student loans.

Today I was dressed as Little Red Riding Hood. It was Saturday morning in late September, and the Halloween season was in full swing. We always dressed up on the weekends during the Halloween season.

I went to the display case and pulled out the tray of cinnamon fudge. It smelled heavenly, and I couldn't wait until the customers were gone so I could snitch a piece. I cut off a slab that looked to be about a quarter of a pound and weighed it for my customer and then did the same with the peanut butter fudge.

"I'm going to have trouble controlling myself and not eating it all at once," the woman said.

"I have the same problem," I said.

My mother came in from the back room carrying a tray of candy corn marshmallows. She had been working on the recipe for more than a week to get the flavor and texture just right. I had tasted one earlier, and it was going to be a heavenly addition to the candy we sold.

"Hello, there," she sang out to my customer. "How are you this morning?"

The customer I was waiting on looked up and smiled at her. "Hello, I'm fine. I just love your fudge. This is my first visit this season, but I've come every year for the past three years. I don't remember you having cinnamon fudge last year."

"I haven't made it for a few years, probably before you started coming regularly," Mom said, heading to the display case. "We just love return customers. I hope you keep visiting."

"You know I will," she said, having forgotten about the curse. Great fudge does that to a person.

I wrapped up her fudge and took it to the register. "Was there anything else I can get for you?" I reached for a cute little jack-o'-lantern print paper bag to put the candy in.

She shook her head. "No, I think that's all for now. I'll be bringing my grandchildren with me next weekend. I can't wait to see the looks on their faces. They'll be visiting from Ohio, and they've never been to Pumpkin Hollow."

"How exciting," I said. "I know they'll enjoy visiting. Don't forget to stop back in and let them pick out their favorite candy."

"Oh, I will," the customer said.

"Mia," Mom said, carefully placing the candy corn marshmallows into the display case. "I've got some chocolate pumpkins setting up in the back. I think I'll make some taffy, too."

"That sounds great," I said as I rang up the woman's purchase. The woman paid for her purchase, and I handed her the paper bag with her fudge in it. I thanked her as she headed for the front door.

There were three other customers in the store, but they were all busy looking over the candy on the shelves. Thankfully, none of them seemed interested in the talk of a curse on the town.

I heard the tone on my cell phone signaling a text, and I reached under the counter for it. It was from Ethan Banks.

If you're free for a minute, can I stop by to talk to you?

I texted him back: *Yes of course. I'll be here.*

My stomach did a little flip. Before I had left for college, I had lived my whole life in Pumpkin Hollow. Ethan hadn't been a friend of mine in high school, but we had become friends since I had moved back. In fact, we were becoming more than friends. We had gone out on two dates, and I hoped there would be many more.

"Ethan?" Mom asked.

I nodded and grinned, feeling foolish. But I couldn't help it. It was Ethan, after all.

I rang up two more customers, keeping one eye on the front window, looking for the police squad car to show up. Ethan was on the Pumpkin Hollow police force, and it seemed like he was on my mind all the time lately. I spent a lot of my day trying to come up with reasons to drive past his house. Ethan probably didn't know it yet, but he had his very own stalker.

When the squad car pulled up to the curb out front, I looked over at my mother, who was rearranging a shelf of foil-covered candy ghosts and skeletons.

"Mom, do you mind if I step outside for just a minute?"

Mom looked up at me and smiled when she saw Ethan's car at the curb. "Of course not, you don't want to keep Ethan waiting."

"Thanks," I said and headed to the door.

Ethan had just stepped out of his car when I walked outside. I went to him and smiled, suddenly feeling shy. I probably looked like a grinning fool, but I couldn't help myself. The Little Red Riding Hood costume probably added to that effect.

"So, how are you?" I asked, trying to figure out what to do with my hands. I settled for crossing my arms in front of myself.

Ethan grinned back and brushed his blond hair off his forehead. "I'm fine. A little tired, though. A couple of officers called in sick, so I worked a night shift on top of my regular shift. You make a cute Little Red Riding Hood, by the way."

I giggled and brushed back the long strand of brown hair that had escaped my headband. "Thanks. You must be exhausted," I said, leaning against his patrol car. Ethan had been the most popular boy in high school, and with his blond hair, blue eyes, and athletic build, he had made many a teenage girl's heart flutter.

"Yeah, I'm really tired, but at least I'm off work now. I just thought I'd stop by and say hello to you before I went home and conked out for the day."

"That's so sweet of you," I said. I wanted to reach out and touch his hand, but it felt awkward. We weren't at the randomly touching stage yet. At least, I didn't think we were. "How have you been doing?" I had just seen him the day before, but it felt like ages since I'd laid eyes on him.

"I'm doing great. You look good in red," he said with a chuckle.

"Don't you tease me," I warned. I loved dressing up every weekend during the Halloween season. It was one of the things that I had always looked forward to when I was a kid, along with helping my mom and dad at the candy store. Dad had a job selling insurance these days, but my mom was still making and selling candy.

"Okay, I won't tease you, I promise. Why don't we go out to dinner again? Sometime soon?" he asked, looking deep into my eyes. "I'm kind of beat right now, so I don't know that I could manage to be coherent tonight. But, soon?"

"That sounds like a great plan to me," I said softly.

As we stood talking, Ethan's radio went off. A call came in about an accident at the haunted house over on Goblin Avenue, calling for all available officers. Ethan looked at me. "Well, I thought I was on my way home," he said tiredly. "But I guess I'll head over to the haunted house and see what's going on." He glanced at his watch. "They're getting ready to open in about ten minutes."

"I hope it isn't anything serious," I said, but since all available officers had been called, I knew that probably wasn't the case.

"I'll call you later, Mia," he said, and opened the driver's side door and got in. On a whim, I ran over to the passenger side door and got in beside him.

Ethan looked at me, questioning. "What are you doing?"

"You don't mind if I ride along, do you?" I had made a quick decision, and I hoped he wouldn't say no.

He considered it for a moment. "I guess it's okay. Citizens do ride-along sometimes," he said. "But I need you to stay in the car."

"Good, I was hoping you would say that," I said. We had had two murders and an arson fire in the past month, and something about this call set my Spidey senses to tingling. For a town with family-themed attractions, things hadn't been very family-friendly lately, and I wanted to know what was going on. Pumpkin Hollow couldn't stand another scandal.

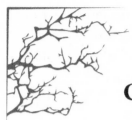

Chapter Two

WHEN WE PULLED UP TO the haunted house, there was a long line of customers waiting to get in. The haunted house was one of the town's most popular attractions. It had originally been a Victorian mansion with a tall clock tower, built in the late 1800s. It had been vacant for years when the town took on the Halloween theme, and the then owner transformed it into a haunted house. The house has had several upgrades through the years and the current owner, Charlie McGrath, tried to change up the scary scenes on the inside every year to keep it interesting.

Black spider webs clung to the corners of the dusty windows, and a large furry stuffed black spider made its way down the front porch wall. The clapboard siding was a peeling white-turned-gray color that added to the creep factor, and a wrought-iron fence surrounded the property. The gates were now wide open to accommodate tourists.

There was an actor dressed as a witch walking around out front of the house greeting the guests, and a zombie made an appearance now and then at the corner of the house, peeking around at the tourists waiting to be let into the haunted house.

A couple of the smaller children looked frightened every time the zombie poked his head around the corner, but the accompanying adults just laughed at it.

Ethan parked the patrol car on the side of the house, and we got out. Gary Collins was an actor wearing a stovepipe hat and a tattered black tuxedo who paced back and forth on the wrap-around front porch near the still closed front door. His white grease-painted face showed worry. The black eyebrows he had colored in exaggerated his features, making him look more frightening than he otherwise might have. Whatever had happened, I was glad it occurred before the guests were allowed inside the attraction.

Ethan was the first police officer on the scene, but another police car pulled up behind his car and parked. I followed Ethan onto the front porch and up to where Gary kept watch.

"Gary, what's going on?" Ethan asked.

"I don't want to talk out here in front of the guests," Gary whispered, glancing at the long line of people waiting for the haunted house to open. An ambulance pulled up as we headed to the front door and a murmur went through the crowd.

Gary unlocked the door and let Ethan, myself, and the two other police officers who had joined us inside the house. As we walked through the doorway, we could hear murmured complaints from the people behind us in line. Gary waited and held the door open for the EMTs, then shut it behind them and locked it.

He turned around and looked at us wide-eyed. "There's been, I don't know how to say this, but an accident?" he said sounding unsure. "When the actors came in this morning and got into their places, they found him. Follow me."

Ethan glanced at me. "Maybe you should stay here, Mia."

"I'll be okay," I said, trying not to sound nervous. What Gary said sounded ominous, and to be honest, I wasn't sure if I would be okay. But I was about to find out.

We followed Gary through the dimly lit haunted house. The lights had been turned up, but they weren't very bright, and it took a minute for my eyes to adjust. There was just enough dim lighting that we could see the path that passed the graveyard, the mad scientist room, and a pumpkin patch filled with goblins. Then we headed toward a cave where an actor playing a caveman usually stood.

"Do you see what I see?" I said to Ethan.

He slowed his pace as we all looked up at the wall above the cave.

"Yes, I'm not sure what happened here, but I can assure you that that was not there when we locked up last night," Gary said over his shoulder.

Graffiti had been spray-painted in neon green and black letters on the wall above the cave. The death threats drawn in large letters spilled across the wall and onto the fake rock cave.

"That's frightening," I said, staring at the writing on the wall.

In front of the cave entrance was a small abutment of faux stone that the caveman usually stood on while grunting and growling at passing guests. He would occasionally reach out to touch a guest in hopes of getting a fearful reaction from them. Now a man was laying on this abutment, not moving. Laying across the man's legs was the mannequin caveman that usually stood in the background nearer the cave entrance.

Joe Small was the actor that played the caveman, and he was standing off to the side in his leopard-print caveman suit. He looked at us wide-eyed when he saw us approach. Even in the dim lighting, I could see his face was pale as he headed over to Ethan.

He pointed to the man lying on the floor. "I just came in this morning to take my place here at my station, and this is what I found," he said before anyone could ask him what happened.

From where I stood, I could see a spear sticking out of the man. It was an odd sight, and it made the hair on the back of my neck stand up. I wasn't close enough to see who it was laying there. Ethan walked over to the body and crouched down near his head. The other two police officers followed him, standing over the body.

I wasn't sure if I should follow Ethan or not, so I moved just a little closer. I didn't know how much I wanted to see, but out of the corner of my eye, I saw the spear was stuck into the man's chest, and the man wasn't moving.

"It's Greg Richardson," Ethan said to the other officers, looking up from the body in the dim lighting.

"Yup, sure looks like him," Officer Sam Chou said.

Officer Chris Denny knelt down beside the body and placed a hand on his neck. "He's long gone."

I took a few steps closer and leaned over just a bit so I could get a look at his face. He was turned toward me, and his eyes were open. He looked stunned. Whoever had done this had taken him by surprise. I suddenly felt nauseous, and I took several steps back, turning away.

I didn't know Greg Richardson well, only that he owned a lot of rental houses in Pumpkin Hollow. His wife Veronica stopped in at the candy shop regularly. She was addicted to my mother's fudge.

Ethan looked over at Gary. "Something has to be done about the crowd outside. He's dead, and we can't let anybody in here until we take a look around."

Gary shook his head. "I don't know what we're going to do," he said. "People come from all over to see the haunted house. What am I going to tell them?"

"Tell them the attraction isn't functioning properly," Sam said. "They don't need to know any details, and we aren't going to give them any right now. Tell them it will open up as soon as possible."

"I seriously doubt this place is going to be open today, or even this weekend," Chris said.

"I know," Sam said. "But if people know there's been a murder, they'll hang around asking questions."

Gary took a couple of steps closer to the body and peered over at him. "Is there a possibility he just fell on the spear? Maybe it was an accident?"

"I really don't think that's what happened," Ethan said evenly. "He has a spear in his chest, and that would be one heck of an accident. We'll need to investigate, and the medical examiner will make the determination, but we're investigating this as a murder."

Gary sighed and nodded his head. "I know you're right. I'll go talk to the folks outside."

"Gary, is Charlie McGrath here this morning?" Ethan asked before Gary left.

He turned back to Ethan. "No, he usually comes in later."

"Give him a call and ask him to come in right away, will you?"

He nodded and left without another word.

Once again I wondered what this town was coming to. Last month, the city council had proposed an initiative to end the Halloween season. The mayor had been murdered, and the town was struggling financially. Some of the town's citizens were behind the initiative to end the season, but it was a tradition going back to the 1940s, and it was what made this town special. We couldn't lose the Halloween season.

Halloween themed businesses occupied two streets in town, with some attractions being here near the haunted house, as well as the haunted farmhouse on the edge of town. We once had a corn maze and a straw maze, but they had burned down recently. Most of the Halloween themed business owners, and I were determined to fight to keep the season going, but a third murder wasn't going to help sway the vote to keep the season alive. And now one of our best and most popular attractions was going to be closed for who knew how long. I took a deep breath. This was going to be a long Halloween season.

Chapter Three

JOE WAS STILL STANDING off to the side, looking woozy. His arms were folded across his chest in a casual stance, but his pasty skin tone gave him away. "I don't know how something like this could happen. How did he even get in here?" he said to no one in particular.

"That's something we'll have to figure out," Ethan said mildly. "What time did all the actors come in today?"

"Everyone is supposed to be here no later than 9:30," Joe said, glancing at his wristwatch. "But some people seem to think they have their own schedule. An awful lot of them just wander in at the very last minute."

"Did Greg Richardson work here on the weekends?" Ethan asked him.

Working at the haunted house was a part-time gig, and most of the actors had full-time jobs that supported them in addition to the job here at the haunted house.

Joe shook his head. "No. He didn't work here at all."

"Who was the first person here today?" Ethan asked.

"Gary. He always opens the haunted house."

"Did Gary find him?" Ethan asked.

He shook his head. "No, I did when I came over here to take my place." He looked at Ethan. "This is the last thing I expected to see."

"Did you take his pulse?" he asked.

Joe's eyes got big. "No. He wasn't moving, so I figured he was dead. I just called Gary over to see what had happened, and he called 911."

I thought it was odd that he didn't check for a pulse. Even with a spear sticking out of his chest, Greg still might have been alive.

"And I guess he didn't check for a pulse, either?" Officer Chou asked.

He shoved his hands into his pockets. "He did, but he couldn't find one. What does it matter? I thought you said he was long gone?"

"He is. We're just trying to figure out a timeline of what happened," Ethan assured him.

"Joe, how many people have keys to this place?" I asked. One of the other officers looked at me kind of funny. Maybe I should have kept my mouth shut, but I couldn't help myself. I had been working so hard to save the Halloween season, and I felt like all my hard work was going up in smoke.

Joe shrugged. "Only Charlie and Gary. A couple of weeks ago, Charlie collected all the keys from everyone except Gary."

"Why did he collect all the keys?" Ethan asked him.

"Because we were having all kinds of trouble with people being in here when they weren't supposed to be. Jake Armand is in high school, and he and his buddies would have make-out sessions here after closing. Kind of as a dare, I guess. They think this place is haunted," he said with a snort and a shake of his head. "Some people aren't real bright."

"How long have you worked here, Joe?" Ethan asked.

"I've been working this gig since I graduated high school twenty years ago. A lot of people have come and gone in that time. No telling if they all turned their keys in. It wouldn't surprise me if half the town had keys."

"That isn't going to be helpful," Ethan said with a sigh. He looked over at me. "Maybe you should call your mom and ask her to come get you? This really isn't a good place for you."

I wrapped my arms around myself and looked at Ethan. "I'll be okay," I said. I tried not to look over at the dead body. "I hope this doesn't hurt the Halloween season more than it's already been hurt." I shouldn't have been thinking about that at a time like this, but I couldn't help it. We'd had more than our share of trouble.

"We'll get the haunted house open as soon as we can." He turned back to one of the other officers, his face grim, and whispered something.

To keep from being noticed and asked to leave, I wandered off and had a look at the other props in the haunted house. I had been in the haunted house several times after hours over the years, and I knew where almost everything was. There were basement stairs in the corner at the back of the main room, and I headed there. I looked over my shoulder. Ethan was busy with the other officers, and the actors were gathered around the entrance, trying to keep out of trouble and most likely gossiping about possible scenarios for why Greg had been killed.

The basement door was closed, so I picked up the edge of my red cape and used it to take hold of the doorknob and turn it without leaving fingerprints. I did it as lightly as I could so I wouldn't wipe away any fingerprints that might be on it.

The basement was dark, so I flipped the switch at the top of the stairs, using the back of my hand. The basement flooded with light, and I shielded my eyes for a few moments until they adjusted. When I removed my hand, my eyes were drawn to a broken window across the room just above ground level. I glanced around the room in case anyone was in there, but the room was empty except for storage boxes and dusty props. I walked slowly down the steps, not using the handrail until I stood in front of the broken window. My eyes went to the floor in front of it. There was very little broken glass. I squatted down to take a closer look at the floor for a moment, and then I stood again and looked at the window. If someone had broken into the haunted house from the outside, most of the glass should have been on the basement floor.

I did a cursory check of the rest of the room but didn't notice anything out of the ordinary. Heading back up the stairs, I heard voices coming toward the basement door. I walked faster, hoping no one objected to me being down here.

Ethan was at the door when I got to the top of the stairs.

"What's going on, Mia?" he asked, his eyebrows furrowed.

"There's a broken window down here. But there's almost no glass on the inside. If they broke it from the outside, wouldn't the glass be on the inside of the basement?"

"It should be," he said, nodding, and looked past me. "You didn't touch anything, did you?"

"No, I used my cape to open the door and the back of my hand to turn the light on," I explained.

He nodded and held up a clear plastic bag that held a coffee cup from the Little Coffee Shop of Horrors. The edge of the lid had bright pink lipstick on it.

"You think it's from the killer?"

He shrugged. "Could be. Or it could have been left behind by a visitor yesterday. We'll hang on to it, just in case. Let's go back and see if Charlie's here yet. We'll need to dust this room for prints."

"What about that graffiti out there? It's weird, isn't it?"

"It is weird. We'll have to figure out how that fits in with the murder," he said, and we headed back to where the body lay.

Joe was now pacing back and forth near the cave. The worry lines formed indentations across his forehead, and he muttered to himself. He saw me and walked over to where I was. "I just don't how this could have happened," he said, looking at me as if I might have an answer.

"I don't either," I told him. He was becoming agitated, and I wished there was some way to comfort him, but it wasn't like I had any insight into what had happened.

Ethan went over to where the other officers were looking at the body and knelt down next to it, looking closely at the spear in Greg's chest.

"Hey Joe, want to come over here for a minute, please?" Ethan asked.

Joe sighed and moved closer to where Ethan was examining the body but didn't get too close. "Yeah?"

"Take a look at this spear, Joe," Ethan said. "Does it look familiar? You have one lying over there next to where you were standing. How many spears do you have when you're playing the caveman part?"

"I usually just carry one," Joe said. "But there are always a few extras lying around just as props. Sometimes I pick this one up, or sometimes I pick that one up. It doesn't matter which one I use if you want to know the truth."

Ethan looked up at him from where he was kneeling. "Can I see that spear over there?"

Joe went over and picked up a spear lying on the floor and brought it to Ethan. Ethan examined the spear, turning it over in his hand.

"This one is made of plastic, isn't it?" Ethan asked.

"Yeah, or something similar," Joe said.

Ethan reached over and ran a finger along the shaft of the spear that was sticking out of Greg's body. "This one is made of wood. Does this spear look familiar to you? Do you have both wood and plastic spears?" Ethan asked.

Joe grimaced and forced himself to focus on the part of the spear sticking out of Greg's body. "I've never seen that one before. Most of the spears are cheap and lightweight, like this one. They're just props and aren't meant to be used."

Ethan looked at me, his eyebrows furrowed in thought.

It was odd that the spear used as a murder weapon wasn't one normally lying around the cave. It begged the question—who carried a spear around with them? Had they carried it into the haunted house with the intent to kill someone?

Joe stepped away from the body and came to stand next to me. "I know it was Charlie," he whispered.

I turned to look at him. "What makes you say that?" I asked.

"He and Gary were the only ones with keys. And I happen to know Charlie didn't like Greg."

"Why didn't he like him?" I asked.

He shrugged. "I don't know. A few weeks ago, I overheard Charlie say his name and start swearing."

I considered this. It was too early to know what the motive for the murder was, but it was something to keep in mind.

Chapter Four

IT HAD BEEN AN HOUR since Charlie McGrath, the owner of the haunted house, had been called but he still hadn't shown up.

Ethan came and stood beside me. "The coroner just got here. This is probably going to take a while."

I nodded. "I know I already said this, but this isn't good for the Halloween season." I whispered it so no one would hear me. I wasn't proud of myself for being so concerned about business when a man was lying dead not twenty feet away, but there were a lot of jobs at stake. We had had a lot of trouble the previous month when the mayor was murdered, and now we had another dead body.

"I understand exactly what you're saying," Ethan said. "We'll get through this. Why don't you go out front and see how things are going with the crowd?"

"All right," I said, trying not to sound worried.

Gary was sitting on the wrought-iron bench out in front of the haunted house. His head was in his hands, and he didn't look up when I approached.

"How are things going out here?" I asked.

"About as well as can be expected," he answered without looking up. "This is going to hurt the season, isn't it?"

I sighed and sat on the bench beside him. The crowd had thinned out, and there were only a couple of stragglers still hanging around. "It is, but I'm sure the police will try to get this place opened up as soon as possible. They know how important it is to the town, and I'm sure they'll figure out what happened in there."

Pumpkin Hollow was a small town, and everyone knew everyone else. I even recognized many of the tourists because the Halloween season was so popular, and we got a lot of repeat customers. Who would have had a reason to kill Greg Richardson? That was the question of the day.

I looked up as a group of three teenaged boys approached the house.

"I'm sorry kids," Gary said, looking up at them. "The haunted house is closed for now. We'll open up as soon as we can."

The kids groaned and muttered their disappointment.

Then the one that looked the oldest, said, "What do you mean it's closed? First, the corn and straw mazes burn to the ground, and now this. There isn't anything fun to do in this town anymore."

That was exactly what I didn't want to hear. At this rate, if we lost any more attractions, the Halloween season would be a complete bust, and we wouldn't have to worry about the city council canceling the Halloween season. With a lack of attractions, the tourists would cancel it by not coming. Something had to be done.

"Sorry, kids," I said as they wandered off.

"This is terrible," Gary said, staring at his boots. Then he looked at me, worry etched in the lines of his face. "Can I tell you something?"

I nodded. "Yes."

"Promise you won't tell anyone? Especially not Charlie?"

I bit my lower lip. I hated making a promise I might not be able to keep. "Maybe you better tell me first."

He sighed, his shoulders lifting and sagging with the effort. "Charlie told me to change all the locks when he collected the keys from the employees a couple of weeks ago. And I didn't do it."

"Wouldn't he already know that if he had one of the old keys? Seems like he would have expected you to give him a new key when you had the locks changed."

He shook his head. "Charlie never opens the haunted house himself. He wanders in at some point during the day, but he's never here early. It's always me. I know he never even realized I hadn't given him a new key. Before we caught those kids in the haunted house after hours, he used to give out keys pretty freely to the employees. I bet most of the employees that worked here over the years had a key. Most give them back when they quit or are fired, but I know not all of them did. Maybe it was one of them that killed Greg."

The thought sickened me. We could be looking at any number of possible suspects. "I guess it's possible. But they would have to have some sort of motive to kill him. I think it's too early to know anything; we need to wait for the police to investigate," I said, hoping to assuage at least some of his fears.

He nodded slowly and went back to staring at his boots. "I suppose you're right. But if I had changed the locks when I was supposed to, there would be a lot fewer suspects."

He was right. But at this point, we didn't even know if the killer had used a key to get in. "Do you think Charlie might have done it?" I asked. I wondered what his thoughts would be about that.

He looked at me and considered it, then shook his head. "I can't imagine why he would. Charlie is pretty laid back most of the time. I can't see him murdering anyone."

"That's what I thought. Don't worry, Gary. It won't do you any good to let your imagination run away with you. Let the police work on this," I said, squeezing his arm.

"Yeah, I know you're right," he said without looking at me.

I wandered back into the haunted house. Some of the other actors were standing around talking to one another, and I walked up to one of the mummies.

"Hi, Steve," I said. Steve Jones had been in the drama club in high school, and since he never made it to Hollywood, it was fitting that he spent his weekends acting in the haunted house. "Do you know anything about what happened here?"

Steve shook his head and pushed up the flap of dingy white fabric that covered his mouth so he could speak. "I have no idea. I came in late, just after the police got here. Gary told me what happened. So, it's Greg Richardson?"

"It is," I said. "I don't know who would want to murder him."

He snorted. "He's a slumlord. I expect there are a lot of people that would want to murder him."

A zombie wandered over to where we were standing. It took a few seconds before I realized it was Sarah Johnson. Sarah was the daughter of one of my mom's friends. "Joe and I walked through the entire house last night after we closed," she volunteered. "We made sure no one was left behind. I don't understand how that guy could have gotten in here."

"You guys check every room and every nook and cranny of this place before you leave every night?" I asked. It made sense to do it, but I could also see where it might not get done every night. Someone might have wanted to leave early, or they might have only checked part of the floor.

She nodded. "Now and then some of the teens decide to hide away in here. They dare each other to stay the night in the haunted house, so we have to make sure everybody is cleared out. We did exactly that last night, and I know for a fact this place was empty."

"What time do you guys close at night?" I asked.

"We close at midnight on Fridays and Saturdays. Sundays we close at ten," she said.

Even with all the attractions during the Halloween season, the sidewalks and streets were pretty much cleared by 12:30 a.m. On the weekends, we didn't have much of anything else going on besides the Halloween attractions. We had a couple of bars that stayed open until 2 a.m., but they were on the other side of town.

"Who locked the doors last night?" I asked. The broken window in the basement didn't make sense, so I didn't ask her about that. She would have surely brought it up if she had seen it.

"Gary did. He worked the earlier shift, then came back to lock up since Charlie doesn't want us to have keys anymore."

"Okay, thanks for the information," I told her and headed back to where Ethan was.

"This is crazy," Ethan said when I got to him.

I nodded. "I asked a couple of people out front about what happened," I said. "No one knows how he could have gotten in here. Sarah Johnson said they clear the house every night before they lock up. She said they check thoroughly every night because of the kids trying to stay after hours."

As we were talking, Katrina Hill walked up to us. She was the witch from out front. "Hey, Mia. Ethan, can I tell you something?"

Ethan nodded. "Please, go ahead."

"I know I probably shouldn't say this," she said and looked over her shoulder. "But Frank Garcia got fired right before the start of the Halloween season. He worked here last season and was a real troublemaker. I didn't think Charlie would hire him back for this season, but for some reason, he did. Then he got fired because he was such a flake and didn't show up half the time. I just thought I'd throw that out there to you."

"Why do you think he might have something to do with the murder?" Ethan asked.

She shrugged. "I don't know, it's a feeling I get. Maybe I shouldn't have said anything. I don't know anything definite, but the guy was a real jerk. He was always goofing off, always late. Sometimes he didn't come in at all. When Charlie fired him, Frank swore at him and said he would get him back. He's working down at Pizza Town now. Maybe you should look him up."

Ethan took his notebook out and made a note of it. "Have you seen him since he was fired?"

She opened her mouth to answer, then glanced over her shoulder. Charlie had finally arrived and approached us, his face pale, and his eyes bloodshot. He looked at us and forced himself to smile.

"Excuse me," Katrina said, and nodded at Charlie, then disappeared among the props.

"Ethan," he said, sticking his hand out.

Ethan shook it, and then Charlie offered me his hand.

"Sorry, I'm late. I overslept," Charlie said, looking embarrassed. "I'm usually the first person here."

The first person here? That wasn't what Gary had said.

"Not a problem, Charlie. I guess you're aware that Greg Richardson was found dead here this morning?"

He gave a short nod. "Yes, I've been told. I don't understand how he got in here."

"Does Greg come by the haunted house much?" I asked.

He shrugged. "I suppose he's been here a few times. I see most of the locals now and then, just like every other Halloween business does."

"Do you have any idea who might have done this?" Ethan asked. "Have you spoken to Greg recently?"

"No, I can't remember when the last time was that I spoke to him. I'm completely puzzled as to why he was killed here.

Although," he said after thinking about it, "I did fire Frank Garcia a few weeks ago, and he threatened to pay me back."

Ethan glanced at me. "Do you think he would pay you back at Greg's expense?"

It seemed like an odd conclusion for Charlie, as well as Katrina, to jump to, and by the look on Ethan's face, I was pretty sure he felt the same way.

Charlie's eyes were on the far wall behind the caveman exhibit. "Maybe. Maybe not. But I can tell you one thing I know for sure," he said. "He's been in here. He has a police record for vandalism. I caught him tagging the cinder block wall outback a week ago."

Ethan looked at the wall. "Did you report him when you caught him vandalizing the wall out back?"

He shook his head. "No, I just ran him off."

"I can check into his criminal record," Ethan said.

Charlie ran the back of his hand across his forehead. "I hope you check into a lot of things where he's concerned. He was nothing but trouble."

"I'll certainly look into it," Ethan assured him.

"How long do you think the haunted house will have to be closed?" he asked, looking over to where Greg lay.

"I can't really answer that question right now," Ethan said.

He nodded without looking at Ethan. "I guess that makes sense." Charlie watched as the coroner examined Greg's body. His hands clenched and unclenched at his side, and there was a sweat ring around the neck of his t-shirt. The weather was cool at sixty-five degrees with a breeze that had been blowing all morning. It seemed odd that he would be sweating so profusely.

"We'll do our best to get the haunted house open as soon as possible, but no promises at this point," Ethan informed him.

"I appreciate that," he said. He suddenly turned to look at Ethan. "Do you mind if I have a look at him?"

"Sure," Ethan said with a nod and watched as Charlie slowly walked over to take a look at Greg.

Ethan raised his eyebrows at me. I shrugged.

"I don't know what's happening with this town," I said. "What happened to the sweet town we knew as kids?"

He chuckled. "I guess things change whether you want them to or not. We'll get to the bottom of this. Don't worry. For now, why don't you go back to the candy shop? I've got to hang out around here and question people. Boring stuff. I'll give you a call later today."

"You need to go home and get some sleep," I said. The dark circles under his eyes were becoming ominous.

He gave me a tired smile. "I promise I'll go home soon. I'll give you a call after I take a nap."

I didn't want to go, but I didn't want to be in the way, either.

"Okay, I'm going to go back to work. I'll talk to you later." I stood for a moment too long, wondering if he might give me a quick kiss goodbye. When it didn't happen, I pasted a smile on my face. "See you later."

"I'll see you later," he promised.

The candy shop was only a few blocks away, so I decided to walk, and as I went, I said goodbye to the people that were still hanging around in the haunted house. The worries of Pumpkin Hollow and all the problems that we'd been having lately weighed heavily on my mind, and I wondered if we were ever going to catch a break.

Chapter Five

ETHAN HAD PROMISED he would call me when he got done at the haunted house, but he never did. I kept reminding myself that he had a job to do, and he had to be exhausted from working so many hours. I found myself thinking about Ethan a lot lately. I realized I wanted a relationship, and I hadn't wanted one in a long time.

When I still hadn't heard from him by Sunday morning, I dressed in my black cat costume and went to work, trying not to be too frowny. Our part-time employee, Lisa Anderson, had gotten to the candy shop before I did and was busily stocking shelves with candy when I got there. Lisa was a high school student and was cute as a button in her pink fairy costume and a long blond wig.

Mom and I worked on making candy all morning while Lisa worked at the front counter. We had quite a few customers when the doors opened, and that made me smile despite not getting a phone call from Ethan. I hoped the haunted house was open by now, but I doubted it would be. It took all the self-control I had to keep from texting Ethan and asking about it, but if he had been out late working on the murder, I didn't want to wake him up.

When we had a break from the customers, Lisa went back to work straightening the shelves. As if reading my mind, she looked at me over her shoulder and said, "I know you don't want to hear this, but it's the curse."

I was putting a tray of orange and chocolate bonbons into the display case, and I looked at her. "I really don't believe in any curse. I know things haven't been good around here lately, but that's going to turn around. I just know it is."

"You know, Lisa," Mom said from her place on a stool behind the counter. "Everyone has talked about a curse for as long as I can remember. But no one has ever been able to prove anything. And sometimes talking about this curse can scare the customers off. You know what I mean?"

Lisa nodded. "That's why I didn't say anything earlier when there were customers in here. But I'm telling you, it's the curse on Pumpkin Hollow. My grandmother told me all about it. What other reason would there be for all these murders happening? My friend Tammy Sutton told me there was another murder at the haunted house yesterday."

I had heard about the curse a couple of times when I was younger, but I had completely forgotten about it until Lisa brought it up when the corn and straw mazes burned down. Mom had said there were a lot of people in Pumpkin Hollow that believed a witch put a curse on the town back in the early days when Pumpkin Hollow was founded. Apparently, the witch wanted to live out in the woods by herself and resented that a town was being built right next door to her. But like I said, I don't believe in curses.

"I think it's a really good idea not to bring this up around other people," I said gently. The rumors were already flying, but I didn't want it brought up in the candy shop. We had enough to worry about with business being down and there being another murder.

The candy shop door swung open, and Ethan stood in the doorway. He stopped and looked at me. Then he smiled and walked up to the counter. He was dressed in business casual attire, and that surprised me. I had only seen him in his uniform or jeans and a T-shirt when he was off work. He looked good in his red polo shirt and khaki pants. My heart fluttered in my chest.

"Good morning Mrs. Jordan, good morning Lisa. And good morning, Mia," he said, turning to me. "I'm sorry I didn't call you back yesterday afternoon, but I was exhausted from working the night before, and by the time I was able to get away from the investigation, it was nearly six in the evening. I was so exhausted I went straight to bed and didn't wake up until about an hour ago."

"Wow, that's a long workday. Did you find out anything new about the murder?"

"I wasn't at the haunted house the entire time," he said. "After I did as much investigating as I could there, I went back to the police station. It's too early to know much just yet, but we'll get to the bottom of it."

"It's the curse," Lisa interjected.

He looked at Lisa and smiled. "Maybe we should call some curse busters in? I have no idea who handles that kind of thing."

"It might not hurt to try," she said with a grin.

I chuckled and shook my head. "I just wonder what Greg was doing in the haunted house after hours," I said.

"That's the question of the day," he said. "I do have some news unrelated to the murder." He grinned when he said it.

"It must be good news. Don't keep me in suspense," I said. There was a spark in his still tired eyes that was hard to miss. "What kind of news?"

"I got a promotion. Of sorts," he said, still grinning. "And 'of sorts' is the key phrase here."

"Really?" I asked. "What kind of promotion?"

"I've been promoted to criminal investigator," he said with a grin. "I was kind of surprised about it, to tell you the truth. I had expressed an interest in taking the test to become a detective last year, and I still need to do that, but I didn't expect this."

"Congratulations!" I exclaimed. "I'm so excited for you!"

"Oh, my goodness, Ethan," Mom said. "That's great news. Congratulations!"

"Congratulations!" Lisa chimed in.

"Thanks, everyone," Ethan said, and pink crept up his cheeks. "It really was a surprise to me. But the police chief decided we needed somebody that could investigate the more serious crimes like murder and arson. Unfortunately, as you already know, Pumpkin Hollow has been having more of that kind of thing. I hope my investigative services aren't needed all that often, but as of right now they are."

"What do you mean that it's sort of a promotion?" I asked. It sounded like a normal promotion to me.

"Well, the truth is that Pumpkin Hollow really doesn't have that much crime. Except for the last month or so, that is. So when I'm not needed to investigate the serious stuff, I'll be back on the street in uniform. Kind of a bummer, but the good news is that when I'm investigating, I don't have to wear my uniform." He stood back and held his arms out and turned around for us to admire his clothes.

I laughed. "Well at least that's a positive, right?"

"Indeed, it is," he said. "I can be a real detective once I pass the test, so I'm going to work on that. I want to study for a while before I take the test, though. Maybe then I'll be out of uniform permanently." His blue eyes sparkled in spite of how tired he was.

"I'm really proud of you," I said. "So what's the next step in the investigation?" As soon as it was out of my mouth, I thought better of it. He might be more inclined to tell me key details if there weren't other people listening in.

"We'll be going back over the crime scene again. The problem in the haunted house is that the lights are pretty dim even with all of them turned on. They only needed enough light in there for the actors to find their places," he said.

"I hadn't thought about that," I said thoughtfully. "It was pretty dim in there. Do you know yet how long the haunted house will have to be closed?"

"We're trying the best we can to get it open by next weekend," he said. "I think we can do it."

I was excited and proud of Ethan for getting his new promotion. I also hoped this gave him a little more pull down at the police station. Ethan was happy with his job, but he had mentioned that he wished some things were different. Maybe this would give him leverage to make some changes down there. And maybe that would change some things here in Pumpkin Hollow.

"So what other perks does your new position come with?" I asked.

"I can interview suspects out of uniform," he said, lifting one eyebrow.

I laughed. "Well, I guess that's a perk."

He shrugged. "I seriously doubt I will do it much, but I might. I'm actually on my way down to the station right now, and I've been promised I can work exclusively on the case today. Tomorrow I'll probably be out in my patrol car and in uniform."

"Aren't you tired?" I asked. I didn't want to point out just how tired he looked, but I thought he needed a day off.

He sighed and nodded. "I am beat. But there's a murder to solve, and I don't want the trail to go cold."

"Ethan, you work so hard," Mom said. "Let me get you some pumpkin spice fudge to take with you and help keep your strength up."

"That would be great, Mrs. Jordan. I can't resist your fudge."

Mom went over to the display case and took out the tray of fudge to wrap up a piece of fudge for Ethan. I looked at Ethan and stepped closer to him.

"Is there something I can help you with on the investigation?" I whispered. I knew his boss might frown on that, but I wanted to help.

"Maybe you can ask around and see if anyone knows anything. People might be more inclined to speak to you than to the police. But you've got to be careful how you go about it, and we'll need to keep this to ourselves."

I nodded. "No problem there. I'll see if I can find anything out."

I was about to burst with pride for Ethan. He would make a great detective. I just hoped he could find Greg Richardson's killer quickly.

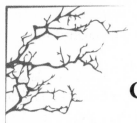

Chapter Six

WHEN I GOT OFF WORK that evening, I went over to Ethan's house. I didn't have any patience left after not seeing him the previous evening, and the few minutes I saw him at the shop wasn't enough. I rang the doorbell and waited, and after a few moments, the door swung open. When he saw me standing there, his eyes lit up.

"Hey Mia, how are you?" he asked.

"I'm fine, Ethan," I answered. "Are you rested up yet?"

"I just got up from a nap a while ago," he said, "and I'm feeling fine as can be."

"I'm glad to hear that, and I was wondering," I said as he held the door open for me, "when are you going to talk to Frank Garcia?"

"I was going over there now. Katrina said he had a job down at Pizza Town. If you're hungry, why don't we go down and have a pizza?" he said.

I grinned. "That sounds like a plan to me."

WHEN WE PULLED INTO the Pizza Town parking lot, it was nearly empty. It was just after seven in the evening, and I wondered if Sundays weren't a very busy night for pizza.

We headed into the restaurant and spotted Frank wiping down tables. He wore a green apron around his waist and sprayed the tabletop with a clear solution from the spray bottle in his hand. We went to him and sat down at the table he was cleaning.

"Hi Frank," Ethan said. "How are you doing?"

"Hi Ethan, Mia," Frank said, looking at us questioningly. "I'm almost finished cleaning this table, but there are a few others that are already clean."

"Actually, Frank, we came to speak to you," Ethan said. "Can you sit down for a minute?"

Frank looked over his shoulder, but he was the only employee in the dining room. A couple of tables on the far side of the room were occupied with customers, but they were out of earshot. He sat down across from Ethan and me. "Sure, I guess so. I didn't get to take my break earlier, anyway. What's up?"

"Did you hear about what happened at the haunted house?" Ethan asked.

Frank's eyes went wide, then he quickly shook his head. "No, I haven't heard a thing. I've been here working all weekend." Frank had black hair and brown eyes with a tattoo of a fiery demon on his left forearm. Frank was two years behind

Ethan and me in school, and we knew him well enough to say hello, but not much more.

"There was a murder at the haunted house, and we heard you worked there until very recently," Ethan said. "Do you keep in touch with any of your former co-workers?"

I studied Frank's face, trying to pick up on anything that hinted at his guilt.

Frank stared at Ethan for a moment, and then he started laughing. "I guess that won't sit well with Charlie McGrath, will it? I can just see that little red-faced runt getting hopping mad over someone having the nerve to die in his haunted house."

"We wondered if you knew anything about it," Ethan said, folding his hands together on the table in front of him. "We also wondered if you knew anything about the graffiti sprayed on the wall behind the caveman exhibit?"

Frank stopped laughing, and his face went pale. "How would I know anything about a murder or graffiti? I don't talk to anyone down there. They're all a bunch of losers. Everyone was afraid of losing their job, so they were always stabbing each other in the back to make themselves look good to Charlie. Me, I didn't care what that runt thought of me. If you want to know the truth, it wouldn't surprise me if Charlie did it himself. Who was killed?" he asked, slouching down in the seat across from us.

"Greg Richardson," Ethan said. "What happened with your job down at the haunted house? Why don't you work there anymore?"

Frank narrowed his eyes at Ethan. "That idiot fired me. I tell you what, I did a good job there. I worked hard. But he didn't like me, and neither did some of the other actors. They were jealous. Some people have a problem with people who work harder than they do. It makes them look bad."

"What kind of work did you do there?" I asked. I thought all the actors did was hang out and try to scare people. It seemed like a pretty easy job, and Frank was saying he worked harder than the others. I just couldn't see how.

"It's more than just jumping out at people, you know? Charlie was always having us cleaning and knocking down cobwebs. I mean, what was he thinking? It's a haunted house! Of course, there's going to be spider webs and dust. I told him he needed to leave it all for ambiance. He just got mad and told me to get to work," he said, shaking his head. "That guy is a piece of work. It's a shame it wasn't him that ended up dead."

I flinched at his words. He had a lot of guts saying that to a cop.

"Maybe he was afraid leaving the spider webs up would encourage poisonous spiders to take up residence in the haunted house," I pointed out.

He rolled his eyes. "Whatever. I told him over and over that cleaning was useless. And then he would criticize the way I played Dracula. I mean, come on, it was Dracula! I stood there and told people I wanted to suck their blood. I flipped my cape around at people. What else was I supposed to do?"

"Did you ask him what else he wanted you to do?" Ethan asked, scribbling in his notebook.

I had often thought I would like to take a job at the haunted house. I could be a zombie ballerina or something. All I would have to do was put makeup on and a torn ballerina costume and groan. How much easier could it get?

"Yeah, he said, I needed to improvise more. He said I was an actor, so I should act. But I was already doing that, so what else was I supposed to do?"

"You know," Ethan said, "I did a little research, and it seems you have a record for vandalism. You spray-painted graffiti on the walls at the high school when you weren't allowed to graduate because you didn't have enough credits."

Frank gripped the edge of the table. "That was a setup. I had all my credits, but Mrs. Livingston said I failed a history test. I didn't fail it. She just never liked me!"

Ethan shrugged. "I don't care if you failed a history test or not. You vandalized the high school and were arrested for it, then you did it again six months later. That's a history of vandalism if you ask me."

"Look, I was a kid then. I did stupid things like all kids do. Don't make this into something it isn't."

"All kids don't commit crimes," I pointed out. "Why did you do it the second time?"

"Because I couldn't get a job without a high school diploma. It made me mad, so one night after having a couple of beers, I stopped by and left my calling card. Again." He sat back and grinned proudly.

"You have a little trouble with letting things go, don't you?" I asked him.

The grin left his face. "I can let things go just fine. I didn't spray graffiti at the haunted house, and I sure didn't kill anyone."

"Did you know Greg Richardson?" Ethan asked.

He narrowed his eyes at Ethan for a moment, then relaxed. "I worked for him last year, cleaning up properties after his tenants moved out. He was a cheapskate. You can't believe the mess some people leave behind, and he expected me to clean up after them for minimum wage." He snorted. "I don't know who killed him, but he had it coming."

"Don't tell me," Ethan said. "You got fired unfairly from that job, too?"

"It *was* unfair. No one should have to do that kind of work for practically nothing. I took pictures of the messes left behind just in case I needed to take him to court. I was still thinking about doing that, but I guess that ship has sailed."

Ethan shook his head. "You got hired to do a job, and you knew what it paid before you took it. Most people do the job or look for something else."

He rolled his eyes. "Whatever. I don't expect a rich kid like you to understand. You've had it easy all your life."

I was shocked he would say that to Ethan's face. Ethan did come from an upper middle-class family, but he didn't have it easy. He'd worked ever since he was old enough to get a job. His family had expected him to go to college and become a lawyer, but he had chosen law enforcement. A police officer's job was anything but cushy.

"You don't know what you're talking about," Ethan said. "Where were you Friday night and Saturday morning?"

"I was right here. Working. Just like I always am. See, some people know the value of hard work, and that's me."

"Your boss will vouch for you?" Ethan asked.

Frank nodded, and his eyes went to an older woman that had just appeared from the kitchen. "Hey, uh, Alice, can you come over here for a minute?" Frank called to the woman.

The woman's eyes went wide, and she hesitated, then walked toward us. Her graying hair was pulled up in a bun, and it was covered in a hairnet. She smiled at us and then turned to Frank. "Yes, Frank?"

"This officer would like to know if I was here at work Friday night and Saturday morning. I told him I was here," Frank said.

She smiled and nodded at Ethan. "Yes, Frank was here until late. We stay open until midnight Friday and Saturday. Friday night we stayed later to do some extra cleaning. Saturday morning we came in early to finish. We've been so busy since the Halloween season started." Her eyes went to Frank as if seeking his approval, and it made me wonder. She wore a plastic name badge that had her first name and the title of assistant manager beneath it.

"Can I get your name?" Ethan asked, making a note in his notebook.

"Alice Gomez. I'm the assistant manager here." Her eyes went to frank again, and he gave her a very slight nod.

"Thank you, Alice," Ethan said and took her phone number down.

Alice went back to the kitchen without another look behind her, and I watched her go. There was something not quite right about what had just happened, but I couldn't put my finger on it.

"If you want to know who I think did it, I think it was Evelyn McGrath," Frank said. "That woman was a piece of work."

"Why do you think she did it?" Ethan asked.

"Because she wanted a divorce from Charlie. She had Internet boyfriends. I know because she left her laptop unlocked in the haunted house office one day. I took a look. And she didn't have just one boyfriend, she had three."

"I don't think having boyfriends is a motive for someone else's murder," I pointed out.

"It is if you want to set your husband up and get him thrown in jail," he said, leaning toward me. "Think about it. If he was framed for murder, he'd go to jail for life, maybe get the death penalty. And she'd be sitting pretty with his business, and free to hang out with whoever she wanted."

"Sounds like you're really grasping at straws on that one," Ethan said.

"You're barking up the wrong tree if you think I had anything to do with a murder," he growled.

"It's still early in the investigation," Ethan said with a shrug. "Someone mentioned you had been fired from the haunted house recently, so I came down here to see what you had to say about it."

"Are you serious?" he asked, shaking his head. "I mean, a dead body shows up, and people are telling you I got fired like there's some kind of connection? Who brought my name up?"

"I really can't go into details," Ethan said. "I'm just following up leads, Frank. Of course, if we find out you are responsible for the graffiti down there, you know you'll be the first to know, right?"

"Yeah, I bet I'll be the first to know," he muttered.

"Frank, do you still have a key to the haunted house?" I asked.

"I never had a key. Only Charlie's favorites had keys. I've been working here six days straight without a day off, so you already know where I've been. My boss already vouched for me," he said, narrowing his eyes at me.

"Fair enough, Frank," Ethan said, putting his hands on top of the table. "I'll make a note of it that you have been at work for six days straight."

"You do that. Make sure all those gossips at the haunted house know that, too. Now, if you'll excuse me, I've got work to do."

We watched as Frank got up, picked up his dishcloth, and headed over to the other side of the dining room.

"What do you think?" I whispered to Ethan.

"We've still got a lot of work to do. I mean, I've got a lot of work to do. Everything that you've heard and seen regarding this case is between the two of us."

I nodded. "I completely understand. I wouldn't want to get you into trouble on your very first day as a detective."

"That wouldn't be a good thing," Ethan said with a grin.

"I noticed Alice seemed to look to Frank for approval of what she was telling us. What do you make of that?"

He nodded. "I saw it too. Maybe she was just nervous talking to a cop. Some people are that way."

"I think we should get dinner somewhere else. Frank's kind of mad at us right now," I pointed out. "I don't want a spitball pizza."

He chuckled and nodded. "Not a bad idea."

We left Pizza Town in search of something else for dinner. I decided for the next hour or so, I wouldn't worry about how things were going in Pumpkin Hollow. The Halloween season was flashing before my eyes, and I desperately wanted things to turn around before it was too late. But for now, I was going to try to enjoy some time with Ethan.

Chapter Seven

THE NEXT DAY I WAS hanging out in Ethan's new office. It wasn't much bigger than a walk-in closet, and the two desks, office chairs, and visitors' chairs took up nearly the whole room. He had to share it with other officers when they needed a place to fill out their reports, but for the most part, it was Ethan's. As I looked around, I considered bringing in some artwork to hang on the walls or some cute little desk accessories, but I wasn't sure how he would take that.

I sat down in a visitor's chair with a sigh. I had spent eight hours at the candy shop making fudge, taffy, bonbons, marshmallows, and pralines. My feet and back ached.

"How do you like my new office?" he asked, sitting back in the black vinyl office chair behind one desk. The chair back had been repaired with black plumber's tape on the side of the seatback.

"I think it's awesome. A couple of pictures on the wall and a plant or two would really spruce things up," I said.

Ethan narrowed his eyes at me. "I was going for the plain and simple look."

I giggled. "Mission accomplished, then."

He began to explain his new responsibilities to me. He was like a little kid that had been given a lollipop the size of his head. He was excited about this new job, and I was excited for him.

"I really am happy for you, Ethan," I said when he stopped talking long enough to take a breath. "This is a great opportunity for you."

"Thanks, I think so too."

"So, has Greg Richardson's family been notified?" I asked.

He nodded. "Veronica Richardson has been in Texas at a conference for her job since Tuesday. She was trying to get a flight back. I had to tell her what happened over the phone."

"That's a terrible way to find out something like that," I said sadly.

Just as Ethan opened his mouth to say something else, the office door swung open. Veronica Richardson walked through the door. Her eyes were red-rimmed, and her mascara had smudged beneath her eyes. I knew Veronica from being a regular candy shop customer.

"Are you the detective in charge?" she asked, looking at Ethan.

"Yes ma'am, I am," Ethan said, standing up and extending his hand. "My name is Ethan Banks."

She walked into the office, which was only a few steps. "The officer at the front desk said this was your office." She glanced at me and then returned her attention to Ethan. "I'm sorry, I barged in. I'm Veronica Richardson. My husband was Greg Richardson. I believe I spoke to you on the phone." Her voice cracked slightly on her husband's name. "Should I come back later?"

I stood up, giving her the visitor's chair in front of the desk, and went around to Ethan's side of the desk. There was an extra chair stuck back in the corner, and I pushed it up a little so I was closer to the desk. I felt awkward, and I wondered if Ethan wanted me to leave the room, but since he hadn't asked me to leave, I didn't.

"No, it's fine. Mrs. Richardson, I'm sorry for your loss," Ethan said. "This is Mia Jordan." He didn't bother saying what I was doing there, so I didn't explain, either.

"I know Veronica from the candy shop. She's a very good customer," I explained to Ethan and then turned to Veronica. "Please accept my condolences on your loss," I said quietly. I didn't know what else to say. I couldn't imagine what she must be going through.

Veronica nodded and looked from me to Ethan. "I don't know what I'm going to do. My husband is dead, and I don't understand why. How did he get stabbed with a spear?" she asked. Tears began streaming down her cheeks, and she rummaged through her purse for a tissue.

"We're still trying to put things together and figure out exactly what happened," Ethan said. "When was the last time you saw your husband, Mrs. Richardson?"

She sniffled. "I tried calling my husband Saturday morning, but I couldn't get ahold of him. I just assumed he was getting in some golf time. He loved to golf, and I could usually find him there when he wasn't at work in his office."

"Do you have any idea what he might have been doing at the haunted house after it was closed?" Ethan asked.

She shook her head. "I have no idea. He never mentioned it to me."

"I see," Ethan said, taking this in. "Did he have a home office you could maybe look through? Maybe he had something on a computer or in a file?"

She shrugged and then nodded. "I can do that. He worked out of his home office. He has a laptop he was never without. None of this makes sense. I just don't understand what happened."

"What did he do for a living?" Ethan asked.

"He owns some rentals and had some investments. They kept him busy enough, I guess," she said, staring at a spot on Ethan's desk, lost in thought for a moment. "I don't know what I'm going to do without him."

"I'm sorry," Ethan repeated. "Maybe you'll find something among his things that will help us figure out what happened."

"I suppose there has to be something somewhere," she said. "I'll take a look, although I don't know what I'm looking for."

"Can you think of anyone that might have had something against him?" he asked. "Had someone threatened him?"

She shook her head. "I can't think of a single person that would do something like this to him. Is there any way this could be some kind of crazy accident?"

"No, I'm afraid not," Ethan said. "I know this is difficult. And again, I'm so sorry for your loss. But we're going to need you to identify the body. You'll need to come down to the morgue."

I inhaled at the word morgue. It was such an ugly word.

Veronica nodded, and her face crumpled. She looked away, and I held a box of tissues toward her. "I'm sorry," I murmured.

"I understand it has to be done," she said quietly. "Let's get this over with."

I could hardly stand to watch Veronica in her grief. Losing someone that you love must be agony. I watched as Ethan stood up and escorted her out of the room to drive her to the morgue.

I didn't accompany Ethan and Veronica. That was more than I could handle. I probably shouldn't have been in his office while he was speaking to her, but no one had asked me to leave, and it seemed less obtrusive to stay. I hoped she could find something in her husband's office that would explain why he was in the haunted house that morning.

Chapter Eight

I WAS PUTTING OUT A tray of pumpkin fudge when Charlie McGrath's wife, Evelyn, walked through the door. I smiled. "Hi, Evelyn, how are you this morning?"

She gave me what looked like a forced smile, her brown curly hair drooping on the sides. She looked tired, and I wondered if the worry of the murder in the haunted house was taking a toll on her.

"I guess I'm as well as can be expected. I hope the police finish up their investigation in the haunted house soon. We're losing money," she said, stepping up to the display case and peering in.

"I don't blame you. The Halloween season needs the haunted house open as badly as you want it opened after losing the corn and straw mazes," I said.

This year's Halloween season had been a disappointing one, and now there was another murder, and the haunted house was closed. I wasn't sure we could handle much else going wrong at this point.

She straightened up and looked at me. "It's not that I'm not sorry Greg Richardson died, you understand, it's just that the haunted house is a large part of our livelihood. Charlie hasn't been doing well selling insurance, and we can't lose another weekend of income from the haunted house."

"I forgot that Charlie sold insurance during the week," I said. Most of the Halloween attractions were closed during the week, except for the week leading up to Halloween. Those jobs were only second jobs for a lot of people.

She nodded. "To be honest, I have to wonder if that insurance company is going out of business. They cut back their employee's hourly pay, expecting them to make it up in commissions." She rolled her eyes. "People have families and homes they need to pay for. I guess they think a pay cut will make them work harder on making those commissions."

"That's a shame," I said and put the last of the fudge into the display case. "I wouldn't think that people buy new insurance policies very often. Once people have their insurance, I would think they would keep it unless they were really dissatisfied in some way."

"I know, right?" she said with a grin. "I think I want some of that pumpkin fudge. I can smell it from here, and it smells delightful. A half a pound, please."

"A half-pound coming up," I said and pulled the tray out of the display case again to cut it.

"If you want my opinion," she said conspiratorially, "I think Joe Small may have had something to do with Greg's death."

My eyes went to hers. "Why do you say that?"

"He's a complainer and a troublemaker. He argues with customers and I told Charlie we needed to get rid of him before he caused any real trouble, but you know how Charlie is. He had some kind of misplaced loyalty toward Joe. He wouldn't get rid of him."

"Oh? He had trouble with the customers?" I asked as I weighed out the fudge.

She nodded. "He did. Two years ago, he got into a fight with a customer that had had one too many beers. He nearly punched him in the face right in front of the haunted house! Charlie had to stop him. I could hardly believe it."

"Wow," I said, taking this in. "Joe has a bad temper?"

She nodded and leaned on the display case. "He does. I mean, sure, the guy was a little tipsy, but it's Joe's job to entertain. He should have walked away from him if he was being obnoxious."

"That doesn't do much for the tourist trade, does it? Actors fighting with the guests?" I asked, wrapping up the fudge and putting it into a cute vintage looking paper bag for her.

"No. He's a nuisance, and he's lazy on top of it. I also heard he rented a house from Greg Richardson a couple of years ago, and he got evicted. It wouldn't surprise me if he got his revenge on him the other night."

I nodded and rang up her purchase, taking this in. Joe may have been evicted from one of Greg's rentals, but would he have been angry enough to lure Greg into the haunted house to kill him? And why the haunted house? Unless it was to try to pin the murder on Charlie.

I looked at her. "Evelyn, someone told me Charlie took all the keys back. If that's true, then how would Joe have been able to get inside after hours? And how would he get Greg to come to the haunted house?"

She shrugged. "My husband thinks he took all the keys back, but let me tell you, that man is a little scatterbrained at times. There were too many keys handed out to employees over the years for him to have gotten them all back. When he demanded them back a couple of weeks ago, he only got four back, and I know for a fact there were a lot more than that duplicated and handed out. Besides, I saw the broken window in the basement when I drove by."

I eyed her but didn't tell her the window was broken from the inside. I was sure Ethan didn't want that getting out. And if there were still keys out there, then anyone could have gotten in. That left why? Why did Greg go into the haunted house after hours with the killer?

"I don't know why Greg would be there after hours, though," I pointed out.

"I don't know either," she said. "That's the thing that bothers me. I just don't get it."

"Evelyn, can I ask you about the haunted house? Is it doing okay financially?" I asked as she ran her debit card through the card reader.

She looked at me sharply, her finger poised above the keypad on the card reader. "Of course it is. We're doing fine. It's just that losing another weekend of the Halloween season will hurt financially. I'm sure you can understand that."

"Yes, of course," I said quickly.

"The haunted house is doing well. It's the most popular attraction in Pumpkin Hollow," she said, tucking her debit card back into her wallet.

"It's one of the biggest attractions," I said agreeably. "I know there are always lines of people waiting to get in."

She nodded. "Mia, I know Pumpkin Hollow is struggling, but I assure you that we are doing fine," she repeated and smiled. "Charlie is so good with business. He's always thinking of things to do differently, to give the customers a little different experience each year. He thought up the caveman display two years ago, and it's been very popular. Next year he said he thought he'd turn it into a zombie caveman display," she said with a laugh. "He's so funny. He's always thinking of things like that."

I chuckled. "That's what we need around here. Someone thinking of different ways to bring more business in."

"Well, I had better get going. Did Ethan mention when he thought they would be done with their investigation?"

"He was sure they would be done with the part of the investigation that's holding up the haunted house before the weekend. I certainly hope so," I said, leaning on the front counter.

"Good. That's what I wanted to hear." She gave me another smile. "Well, as I said, I better get going. Charlie is going to wonder where I got off to. This fudge smells so good, I don't know if I'm going to save him any. You have a good day."

"You too, Evelyn," I said and watched her go.

I wondered if business at the haunted house was as good as she said it was. There was just something that made me think she might not be telling the whole truth.

Chapter Nine

ETHAN HAD A DAY OFF, and I had planned a short hike for us on the goblin trail and then dinner afterward. We parked at Pumpkin Center Park and headed for the four-mile trail that wound through the foothills just outside of town. It was late September, and the weather was crisp, but not cold yet. A fat puffy cloud scampered by overhead as a light breeze blew. The leaves on the trees had already begun changing color, with some trees getting an early start on dropping their leaves.

"It's a beautiful day, isn't it?" I asked Ethan. I had to refrain from reaching out and grabbing his hand. We were walking fairly briskly, and it would be awkward.

"It really is. I love this time of the year," he said, looking at me and grinning.

"Me too. I can't believe how beautiful the trees and mountains are. I think I had a great idea, coming out here for a walk."

He chuckled. "I think it was a great idea, too."

"So what do you think about what we know so far about the murder?" I asked him. He had been working long days since

Greg Richardson had been killed, and I hadn't gotten the chance to talk to him as much as I wanted.

"Not nearly enough. The labs on the coffee cup came back. There were only partial prints on it, not nearly enough for an Id. Not that we could have done much with them, anyway. We still don't know if the cup was from someone walking through the haunted house or if it came from the killer. We'll just hang onto it in case we need it."

"Really? I would have thought someone's prints would have shown up. Whoever made the coffee, and then whoever drank it. What about lip prints? Can you ID someone based on lip prints?" I said with a chuckle.

He smiled. "I doubt it. We could do DNA, but matching DNA isn't as easy as it looks on TV. Once we have a suspect, we can do a DNA test and see if there's a match, but again, we don't know if the cup is significant. Besides, if it is the killer's cup, they may have worn gloves, and the partial fingerprints could be from the barista."

"So we don't know for sure if the killer is a woman or a man yet. It seems like something should have come out of what we know so far, but we've still got nothing," I said.

"The problem with a public place like the haunted house is that there are too many fingerprints. There's no way to tell which ones belong to the killer. There were some partial prints on the spear, but not much else. We're still looking into what we've got."

"Would it do any good to stop in at the Little Coffee Shop of Horrors and see if anyone remembers someone with bright pink lipstick Saturday morning?" I asked wistfully.

He chuckled. "They'd have to have a pretty good memory. Not that it's a terrible idea. Maybe they remember something unusual about a certain customer."

"And if it belonged to our killer, they would have had to come in either Friday night or early Saturday morning. I'll stop by and ask Amanda if she remembers anything unusual. It can't hurt to ask, even if it is a long shot."

"That sounds like a plan," Ethan said as the trail went up a small hill. "This is nice. I don't know why I don't come here more often to get some exercise in."

"I love being outdoors like this. The weather is perfect for hiking," I said. The air was brisk, but the exercise kept us warm enough that we didn't need to wear a coat. Fall was my favorite time of the year, for obvious reasons. But even if I didn't live in a town that celebrated Halloween all year long, I would have loved it. There was something about falling leaves, chilly evenings, and the clean smell of the great outdoors.

"I ALMOST FORGOT, AND I'm afraid to ask," I said to Ethan as we sat at the local steakhouse having dinner after our hike. "But how did things go yesterday?"

Ethan picked up his glass of water and took a sip before answering. He put his glass down and looked at me. "I'm not sure that I like this new position. Taking Veronica to identify her husband's body was one of the hardest things I've ever done."

I nodded. "I don't think I could have done it. It would be too depressing."

"It was actually done by showing her a photograph. She didn't have to see him in the morgue. But it's still a difficult thing to go through," he said.

"It would be hard, no matter how it's done," I said.

"I just hope she can find something among his papers at home that will help us figure out who did it."

I looked over my menu briefly. Then I looked up at Ethan. "Where was his car? How did he get to the haunted house?"

"It was parked behind the haunted house. We've dusted it for prints, but we don't have anything back on them yet. Could be the killer rode over there with him. I think I'm going to have the T-bone steak with sweet potato fries."

"Great choice," I said, looking over the menu. "I just don't understand why he was killed at the haunted house. The obvious choice for his killer is Charlie, isn't it? It's his haunted house. I think I'm going with a cheeseburger and the sweet potato fries on the side. I love sweet potato fries."

"It could be Charlie, but just because it's his haunted house doesn't mean he did it. We have a broken window that was broken from the inside and the graffiti. That bothers me a lot," he said, laying his menu at the edge of the table. He picked up his glass of water again and took a sip.

"Maybe Greg was the person spray painting the wall, and Charlie caught him. A struggle ensued, and he accidentally speared him," I said and laid my menu on top of his.

He chuckled. "That's not a bad theory. But why would Greg break into the haunted house to tag it?"

I sighed. "I don't know. Tell me again, how excited are you about your new promotion?"

He grinned at me. "Well, let me tell you, I am thrilled for this opportunity. The thing is, I didn't get a pay raise with this new job, but I sure did get a lot more responsibility."

"Seriously? I would have thought you would have gotten a pay raise for all the extra responsibility."

"They managed to get out of giving me a pay raise by having me still be a patrol cop when a detective isn't needed," he said, looking at me. "Technically, I'm still just a police officer out on the streets. The chief said they couldn't afford to give me a raise."

"I'm so sorry, Ethan. They really should have done better and gotten you a raise."

He shrugged. "It doesn't bother me that much. I enjoy doing investigations. It's kind of like putting a puzzle together, you know? And it's a lot of good experience that I may be able to take someplace else to make more money, especially after I pass the test to become a detective."

"I'm glad you got it anyway," I said, picking up my glass of tea. "Maybe once you pass the exam, they'll find the money to give you a raise."

He nodded. "Let's talk about you now," he said with a grin. "How are things going for you? I'm glad the website has been doing well, I've been on it several times. I like everything you've done with it."

I had created a website to try to bring business back to Pumpkin Hollow with interactive pages for each of the Halloween themed businesses. It was helping, but maybe not on the scale I had hoped for. It needed more work.

"Thanks. I'm enjoying the fact that I'm living back at home. What I mean is, back home in Pumpkin Hollow, not living in my parents' house. To be honest with you, I'm kind of feeling a little like a failure having to live with my parents again." As much as I loved my parents, I was a grown woman at twenty-eight, and I needed a place of my own.

"You shouldn't feel that way," he said. "A lot of people end up moving back with their parents for a short period after college. It doesn't mean you failed. It just means you needed to take a little breather from life to sort things out."

I smiled at him. He had a positive way of looking at things. "Thanks, Ethan. I hadn't thought about it that way. But to tell you the truth, I think it's time I started looking for my own place. I love my parents, they're the best. And I love being able to spend a lot of time with my mom, both at home and at the shop. But I do think it's time to get my own place."

"I'll keep my eyes open, and if I see an apartment or house for rent, I'll let you know."

"I appreciate that. Before I left Michigan, I got rid of all of my furniture and nearly everything I own. I don't have much right now, but I don't mind going shopping for furniture and other stuff. Actually, I enjoy shopping. A lot. Getting my own place would be a great excuse to buy things," I laughed.

He chuckled. "Why does that not surprise me?"

I smiled at Ethan. I really liked him. He had grown up a lot since the seventh grade when he told half the student body that I had spiders in my hair and that they liked living there because I smelled. Yeah, he did that.

"We really need to get some ideas going for the Halloween season," I said. "We've lost two events, three counting the temporary closure of the haunted house, and we need to do some brainstorming."

"I'm pretty sure we're going to have the haunted house up and running by the weekend," Ethan said. "And didn't you mention goat-tying? Maybe you could work on that. Of course, you'd have to round up some goats."

I lifted one eyebrow and looked at him. "We don't have the time to build a fence and bleachers and then round up goats. However, as silly as it might sound, it's not a bad idea. It's perfect for families with little kids and would fit in with the carnival. I've seen it at a couple of rodeos, and everyone seems to have a good time."

"See? That's what I'm saying. You have a lot of great ideas. Maybe you should work on that for next year, and I mean that seriously."

"I just might do that," I said, thinking about it. We hadn't had a new event in years, and something more for the families was just what we needed.

The waitress came and took our orders. We sat and stared at each other for a few minutes, with very little talking, but I didn't care what anybody thought. I was on a date with Ethan Banks, and I was happy.

We were still waiting to vote on the Halloween season, and even though we had another murder on our hands, when I was with Ethan, I felt like everything was going to work out.

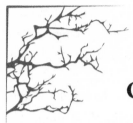

Chapter Ten

THE NEXT DAY I WANDERED over to the haunted house. I was surprised to see Joe Small sitting on the bench out front. The house was still closed, and I really hadn't expected to see anyone there; I had just wanted to get some exercise on my break.

"Hey, Joe," I said and took a seat next to him on the bench. "Are they opening up the haunted house soon?"

"Supposed to open this weekend," he said, not looking at me. "I'm just waiting for Charlie. He's going to bring our checks by. I guess I'm a little early."

"He doesn't do direct deposit?"

"Nope. Charlie's cheap, and I'm sure the bank would charge him a fee to set it up. He isn't going to pay for that. He'd rather have all his employees make a trip to our banks to deposit our checks," he said and took a sip from the cup of coffee he held in his hand. Joe was nearing middle age, and his light brown hair was thinning on top. He always had the appearance of being tired.

"That's inconvenient. I didn't know banks charged for direct deposit," I said. My mother had set up a direct deposit to have mine and Lisa's check deposited every two weeks, but I thought it was something the bank did to get her business. I had never considered asking her if she was charged for it.

"Yeah, it's very inconvenient for me to have to run down to the bank to deposit my check," he grumbled.

"So, any idea what might have happened to Greg Richardson?" I asked casually. He had already pointed his finger at Charlie, but I wondered if he would say anything more.

"Like I said before, it was Charlie," he said without elaborating.

I looked at him sideways. "Why do you say that?"

He shrugged. "It's his haunted house. How else would Greg have gotten inside? Charlie told Gary to take everyone's key back. Of course, it's not like Charlie ever knew how many keys were out there, to begin with," he said with a snort. "Charlie is the most disorganized person I ever met. There's just something about Charlie I've never trusted. If I were a betting man, I'd bet on him."

I considered this for a moment. It was odd that Greg was killed in the haunted house, and Charlie was the owner, after all. But what motive did he have? Joe just sounded bitter to me.

"So, the haunted house was searched before closing late Friday night, right? Did you go straight home afterward?"

He glanced at me. "Yeah, it was searched. I went straight home because I have to be up delivering newspapers at six a.m. on Saturday morning. If Charlie weren't so cheap, I wouldn't have to work four jobs just to make ends meet."

I couldn't understand Joe blaming that on Charlie. The haunted house was a seasonal part-time job at best. How could he expect to eliminate one of his other part-time jobs, even if Charlie paid his employees a little more money? There just wouldn't be enough money to go around, and Charlie needed to make a profit.

"It just doesn't make sense that Greg was here in the haunted house if everyone went home," I said thoughtfully. I wanted to bring up what Evelyn said about Joe getting evicted from one of Greg's houses, but I wasn't sure how to do it.

"Me and Sarah Johnson closed up and checked the rooms. Gary showed up at the last minute to lock up since we didn't have a key. Everyone else was already gone."

"I just hope this thing gets settled quickly," I said.

"Have you heard anything new about whether the city council is going to vote on keeping the Halloween season? I also work at Little Coffee Shop of Horrors. Two of my jobs depend on the Halloween season. It would be just great if they shut the season down, I'd be out of two jobs then," he said dejectedly.

"We'll hear for sure next week," I said. "I didn't know you worked at the coffee shop. Amanda and Brian are friends of mine."

"I started last week. I just do some cleanup during the week and help out where I can. It's not too many hours, but I do get paid a little more than I do here. Can you believe that? I've been here twenty years, and I've only gotten raises when the state minimum wage goes up," he snorted again and shook his head.

"Amanda and Brian are good people. I'm glad you found a job there," I said, trying to stay noncommittal about the pay here at the haunted house. It was obviously a sore spot with him.

"Yeah, they seem nice. I just wish I could find a full-time job, so I don't have to work so many part-time jobs."

"It can be challenging working different jobs," I agreed. "I did a lot of part-time work while in college. It's rough. Some years I had some real financial challenges."

"Yeah, me too," he said mildly.

"I'm considering moving out of my parents' house now," I said. "Do you know if the Pumpkin Hollow Apartments are still nice to rent?" I knew that Greg owned those apartments, and I was hoping he would comment on that.

He looked at me. "Greg Richardson owned those. They're overrun with bed bugs. You don't want to rent one of those."

"Oh, I wouldn't want to deal with bedbugs," I said. "Are you sure about that?"

He nodded. "Oh yeah. I rented one of those last year, and the place was filthy with the nasty things. I kept telling Greg he needed to get someone in there to get them exterminated, but he refused to do it. Said it was my imagination. I asked around the complex, and the other tenants had them, too. So, I refused to pay my rent. By law, he was responsible to get rid of them, and he wouldn't do it."

"What happened then?" I asked.

"He evicted me!" he said angrily. "Can you believe that? It's the law that he gets rid of bugs and rodents, and he was too cheap to do it. Children were living in some of those other apartments, and I saw the bug bites on their arms and legs. But he didn't care. He wouldn't do anything about it."

"Wow," I said. The shock in my voice was genuine. I'd heard bed bugs were almost impossible to get rid of, and if Greg was aware of them and refused to do anything, then that said a lot about his character. "That's really awful. Did you fight the eviction?"

He shook his head. "I thought about it, but in the end, I decided it wasn't worth it. I didn't like living with those bugs any more than anyone else did. It really sucked though, and I had to get rid of everything that couldn't be run through a hot dryer to kill those things. There's no other way to get rid of them."

"I bet you were angry about that. I know I would be."

He nodded and took a sip of his coffee. "I still get mad when I think about it. I was out a lot of money when I had to replace my furniture and mattresses."

I eyed Joe. Evelyn had been right about the eviction, but she had left out the part about him being driven out by bed bugs. I wondered if Joe was angry enough to kill Greg over it. If Evelyn was also right about his temper, then he just might have been.

Chapter Eleven

I WAS RUNNING ERRANDS for my mother and myself the next day on the far side of town. I was so entrenched in Halloween that it seemed weird to see businesses that weren't yet decorated for the holiday. Everything was ordinary, and it made me feel just a little sorry for the other businesses. I stopped in at the Java Bean coffee shop for some liquid caffeine. I felt a little guilty; like I was cheating on my friends Amanda and Brian, who owned the Little Coffee Shop of Horrors, but I needed coffee.

The line was long, and I went to the tail end of it. I inhaled the scent of freshly brewed coffee while I waited. The woman standing in front of me seemed familiar. I tried leaning to the right a little to see if I could get a better look at her, and she caught me out of the corner of her eye and turned around, looking at me. I smiled big when I realized it was an old friend from high school. Carrie Green had been in my chemistry class in my junior year and several other classes when we were seniors. We had never been very close, but she was a nice person, and we always had something to talk about when we ran into each other.

"Hi Carrie, how are you doing?" I asked.

"Mia, how are you?" she asked and hugged me. "I didn't know you were back in town. When did you get back?"

"I'm doing well, I moved back about a month ago. How have you been Carrie?"

"I'm doing great," she said and scooted up a little as the line moved forward. "You know I got married about six years ago, but you might not know we had twin girls two years ago. They keep me so busy. Sometimes I can't tell if I'm coming or going." She laughed. Carrie was petite at five-feet-two, with blond hair and brown eyes. She wore silver wire-framed glasses and had an upturned nose.

"I had no idea, congratulations! I'm so happy for you," I said. I suddenly wondered if I had stayed in Pumpkin Hollow, would I have been able to say something like that by now? Married with two children. Would Ethan have asked me out if I had come back six years earlier, and would we have been married and have kids by now? I pushed the thought out of my mind. It was silly to think like that. Things were the way they were supposed to be, and I was fine with it.

"Yeah, we had wanted to wait a while to have kids, but you know how things go. I found out I was pregnant one day, and life has been full speed ahead ever since," she laughed. "Of course, it's meant that I have to work two part-time jobs—twins are expensive! But Tom and I have alternating schedules, so one of us is almost always with the girls. And when we aren't, one of our mothers has them."

"Wow, that sounds like a lot of work," I said and scooted up in the line with her. "Where do you work?"

"One of my part-time jobs is at the bank down the street," she said, turning toward me as we spoke. "The other is at Pizza Town. At least we get free pizza for dinner a couple of times a week." She laughed. "It's not gourmet food, but it is tasty."

Pizza Town? "Well, you can't beat pizza," I said. "Carrie, you work with Frank Garcia, don't you? How is he to work with?" I looked over my shoulder to see if anybody was listening, but no one was in line behind me.

Carrie made a face and rolled her eyes. "Oh, you mean the hardest working person on the planet?" She laughed again. "I have to hear over and over how hard he works and how nobody else works as hard as he does. Of course, getting him to come to work is a job all by itself."

My antenna went up. "Really? Because the other day he said he'd been working six days straight without a day off."

She shook her head. "It's more like we've been trying to get him to come to work for six days straight." She said and chuckled again. "To be honest, he has come in for six days straight. But he's only worked two or three hours each day because he's always saying he's sick, or he forgets to come in, and then the boss has to call and make him come in, but yeah I guess he has worked six days straight."

I looked at her. "Wow. Why does the boss put up with him?"

"Because he's the manager's wife's nephew. The assistant manager is the manager's sister and is also Frank's aunt. It's a real family affair up there."

Ah. Frank had just earned himself a spot at the top of my list of suspicious people. But there was the question of why he would want to kill Greg at the haunted house. He had threatened Charlie, but why kill Greg there? Unless he really did resent Greg for firing him from his job cleaning up rentals. And if he could somehow set Charlie up for the murder, he would pay back two people at one time for firing him.

"I guess some people get away with murder, don't they?" I said.

She laughed, and we scooted up another couple of spaces in the line. "Some people do. Why are you asking about him?" she wondered.

I shrugged and tried to come up with an answer without giving away the fact that Ethan and I had talked to Frank about the murder. "My mother is looking for another part-time employee." I left it at that. I didn't want to lie to her, and it was true that my mother was looking for another employee. We had lost one several weeks earlier.

Carrie's face lit up. "I hate working at Pizza Town. Do you think your mother would look at my resume if I sent it to her?"

"Of course she would," I said with interest. "I think that's a great idea. Email it to me, and I'll have my mom take a look at it. She's in charge of all the hiring, and I'm sure she'll remember you from when we were in high school."

"That would be great. Mia, did you hear about the murder at the haunted house?" she whispered.

I nodded. "It's the talk of the town."

"Don't tell anyone I said this, but the haunted house is in foreclosure. The bank I work at holds the mortgage," she said, glancing over her shoulder.

"Really?" I said thoughtfully. "Sounds like a lot of bad luck for Charlie McGrath."

She nodded. "I'm glad I stopped in here for coffee," she said. "I almost passed by, but I suddenly got a craving for coffee. I'm so glad you were here."

"I'm happy about it too," I said. And that was the truth. If she hadn't been here, and I hadn't stopped in, I wouldn't have known that Frank wasn't telling the full truth about being at Pizza Town for six days straight and that Evelyn wasn't telling the whole truth about the haunted house's financial outlook. If Frank was only working two or three hours a day, he had plenty of time to commit a murder. And did an imminent foreclosure on the haunted house play into Greg's death somehow?

I needed to talk to Ethan. He needed to know about both of these things.

Chapter Twelve

THE CANDY SHOP DOOR swung open, and Ethan stepped inside. I was wiping down the front counter, and I turned to look at him. He was wearing his uniform, and a patrol car was parked out at the front curb.

"Whoa, I almost didn't recognize you. Why are you wearing a uniform?"

He came to stand beside me. "I told you I still have to be on patrol sometimes," he said with a grin. "I can't be on patrol and not be in uniform. Someone might think I stole the patrol car if I were wearing a T-shirt and jeans."

"That's kind of a bummer," I said.

He shrugged. "I don't mind. I never expected a promotion anyway, so when I don't have to wear my uniform or patrol the streets, it's a bonus." He turned toward my mother, who was washing the front window. "Hello, Mrs. Jordan."

She turned and smiled at him. "Hello, Ethan, it's a lovely day today."

"It sure is. The weather is beautiful."

"I have some news for you," I whispered to him. "Let's step outside for a minute."

We walked over to the squad car and stood next to it.

"I spoke to Carrie Green, who works over at Pizza Town. She said Frank has worked the last six consecutive days all right, but only about two to three hours each day. It seems that for all of his talk about being the hardest worker in the restaurant, it's really just all talk. His aunt is the manager's wife at Pizza Town, and the assistant manager who we met, is another aunt. Apparently, he gets away with murder."

"Two or three hours, huh? That sure leaves an awful lot of time during the day," he said thoughtfully. "Time he could use to do who knows what."

"That's what I was thinking," I said. "Of course, being lazy isn't a motive for murder."

"No, it isn't. But people only lie to cover up something," he said.

"Someone that would make up something like that sure makes you wonder. Do you think he killed Greg in hopes that Charlie would be blamed?" I asked him.

"I think it's a stretch, but it's something I have to consider," he said.

"Carrie also works at the bank, and she told me the haunted house is in foreclosure."

He looked at me. "That's interesting. It may be another piece of the puzzle."

His radio crackled to life, and a call about a domestic disturbance came over it. "I guess that's my cue to leave. I'll talk to you later, Mia. Thanks for the information."

"I'll see you later, Ethan," I said and watched him get into his patrol car and pull away from the curb.

I headed back into the shop to finish tidying up. Early evenings usually saw a rush of customers as people stopped in after work, and I wanted everything to be neat and tidy.

"How is Ethan?" Mom asked.

"He's great," I said and looked up as the door swung open. It was Charlie. "Hi Charlie, how are things going?"

"Hello, Mia," he said, walking up to the front counter. "Things aren't going as well as they could be, but you know about that already. I don't know what could have happened to poor Greg Richardson. It's just terrible."

I nodded. He seemed properly saddened, but I had to wonder if it was genuine. "The things that have been going on around here are scary. But I'm sure the police will get this thing sorted out soon."

"I certainly hope so," he said, looking over the candy in the display case. "This all looks so good, Mia. I'm glad I don't sell candy because if I did, I'd have a mouthful of cavities."

"After a while, it's not as big a temptation as you might think," I said. "My mother just made some bonbons. I strongly suggest that you give them a try because they're the best I've ever tasted."

"Hello, Charlie," Mom called from across the room.

"Hello, Ann," he said, turning toward her. "I sure hope we can get the haunted house opened soon."

"We all do," Mom said.

He turned back to me. "Why don't you wrap up half a pound of bonbons for me?" he said and looked across at the shelves of prepackaged candy that we had just gotten in. He walked over to the shelf and took a look at it. "My niece just loves orange and chocolate together. I might have to get her some of these ghosts."

"Those are tasty. If she likes orange and chocolate, I think she'll love them," I said, opening the display case.

He picked up a box of chocolate ghosts with orange centers and a bag of candy corn and brought them back over to the front counter and set them down. "I guess I'll try these and the bonbons and maybe a quarter pound of that rocky road fudge."

"You do have a sweet tooth," I said with a chuckle and wrapped the bonbons for him.

"That I do, that I do," he said absently. "Say, Mia, has Ethan mentioned anything about the investigation?"

I glanced at him and then went to the display case and took out the tray of rocky road fudge. "You know, it's just so early in the investigation that I don't think they've gotten far with it yet. I'm sure the police are doing everything they can to figure out what's going on." I cut off a slab of fudge for him.

"I understand," he said. "I know they're trying to get the investigation wrapped up so we can open the haunted house again on Friday. It just concerns me that Greg was killed in my haunted house. I don't even know how he could have gotten in. There was a broken window in the basement, but why would he even want to be in there? It just doesn't make sense."

I weighed out his fudge. "It really is weird that he was in there. There wouldn't be any reason he would have a key, is there?"

He stopped and thought about it. "I can't imagine how he would. I keep a tight hold on those things, you know. I just collected them a couple of weeks ago because people weren't being responsible with them. I can't take the risk of people being in there after hours."

I looked at him. Did he really believe he was responsible with the keys? Or was he trying to cover something up?

"That's important," I said, nodding. "So, Charlie, did you go home after work Friday evening?" I couldn't remember if Ethan had mentioned where Charlie was Friday night or Saturday morning.

He nodded. "I went home around seven on Friday. My wife and I slept in late Saturday morning. Gary usually opens Saturday morning, and we were beat after working all week. It's nice to be able to sleep in once in a while, you know?"

"I know exactly what you mean. Sleeping in now and then is good for the soul." Charlie and Evelyn were alibis for one another, and it made sense, but at the same time, it made me wonder.

He nodded. "This thing has me worried though," he said, leaning against the front counter. "I just don't know what this town is coming to. And I hate that it might scare tourists away. You know how the city council wants to close down the Halloween season. If that happens, what am I going to do for business? No one wants to come to a haunted house out here in the middle of nowhere if there aren't other attractions as well."

"Believe me, I understand completely. This is hurting all the businesses in town," I said and finished ringing up his purchases. "It's been a huge worry for all of us."

He nodded as I put his purchases into a paper bag, folded over the top, and handed it to him. He ran his debit card through the card reader and picked up the bag.

"We do appreciate what the police are doing as far as trying to get this thing settled before Friday. You'll let me know if you find anything out, won't you?" he asked.

"Sure I will, as soon as I hear anything, I'll get back to you," I said.

He turned to go and then turned back at the door. "You know, that Frank Garcia was sure a troublemaker when he worked for me. I heard he's a troublemaker at his new job, too, but the manager is related to him, and he can't fire him. If you want to know the truth, I've always suspected him of doing drugs and stealing to support his habit."

"Do you really think so?" I asked, wondering about the drugs. Maybe Greg was involved in drugs as well, and it was a drug deal gone wrong.

"It wouldn't surprise me one bit if Frank killed Greg," he said. "Well, I guess I better get going. I'm taking this time off with the haunted house closed to do some work around my house. My wife has got a honey-do list thirty-feet long." He laughed as he walked out the door.

"Have a good evening," I called as he went.

I watched him go. I had to wonder if what he said about Frank was true. It felt like Charlie was digging for information, but if he thought he was going to get it from me, I was sure I had disappointed him.

LATER I DROVE OVER to Ethan's house to say hello, but when I got there, his truck wasn't in the driveway. I sighed, and my eye was drawn to movement at the house across the street from his. Someone was inside the house, and they stuck a red *for rent* sign in the window. I parked my car and got out, crossing the street. The door of the little house was open, and I went up the two front steps, stopping to knock on the open door.

"Hello?" I called.

"Oh, hello," a woman said, coming to the door. She had blond hair and green eyes and smiled big when she saw me.

"Hi, I just saw you put the 'for rent' sign in the window. Do you mind if I take a look around at the place?"

"Sure, come on in," she said. "We just got it cleaned up after the last tenants, and it's ready to go."

"It's cute," I said, walking through the living room. "It's the perfect size for one person."

"It sure is. It's only one bedroom, one bath, but it's roomy," she said as I looked into the kitchen. The kitchen had white cupboards and matching white appliances. The linoleum on the floor was in good condition, and I could smell fresh paint.

"I really like this," I said as I went through the rest of the house. "Do you have an application?"

"I sure do," she said and picked up an application from the kitchen counter. "We need to do a credit check after you fill this out."

"Thanks," I said, taking the application from her. It may have been a bit impulsive, but getting my own place had been on my mind for a couple of weeks. Living with my parents was fine, but I enjoyed living on my own. It wouldn't hurt to submit an application, and I could decide if I really wanted it if I got approved. After filling out the application, I said goodbye and went to my car, smiling. It would be fun to live across the street from Ethan.

Chapter Thirteen

I DROVE BY ETHAN'S house after work that afternoon. Ethan was just getting into his car when I drove up. He waved at me, and I parked my car and went to him.

"Hi Mia, I was just going over to talk to Veronica."

"Can I ride along?" I asked hopefully.

"I don't know Mia, I'd hate for the chief to say something about you being with me when I go to talk to people," he said apologetically.

"I can understand that," I said. "But maybe the chief wouldn't have to know. What do you think?" I gave him my best smile.

He grinned. "You're trying to get me in trouble, aren't you? Come on, get in the car, and we'll go talk to her."

Veronica lived in a modest ranch-style house in a quiet neighborhood that featured neatly trimmed lawns and large oak trees in the front yards. Ethan parked the car, and we walked up the sidewalk. Ethan knocked on the door, and we waited while the neighbor's beagle barked at us.

The door swung open, and Veronica stood there with her eyes puffy and red from crying. Her long hair was pulled back in a ponytail, and she wore no makeup. She looked exhausted, and it made me sad to see her that way.

"Hello, Veronica," Ethan said. "We'd like to come in and talk to you if that's okay."

"Yes, of course," she said and stood back for us to enter. "Come in, please."

We walked into the house. The color scheme in the living room was done in neutral colors, and pictures of English cottages hung on the walls. Veronica offered us a seat on the sofa, and she sat on the loveseat across from us.

"I've looked through Greg's office and couldn't find anything mentioning the haunted house. I did find his laptop, but I have no idea what the password to get into it is. I've tried everything I can think of and looked through his desk in case he noted it somewhere," she said, crossing her legs and picking up a bottle of water from the coffee table. "I just don't know what he was doing there at the haunted house."

"Can I take the laptop with me? Maybe someone in our IT department can have a look at it and figure out the password. It doesn't make sense that he was there at the haunted house unless he had some business with the killer."

She considered this for a moment. "No one seems to know anything. I don't understand this at all. I don't know, I—." Her eyes welled up with tears, and she grabbed a tissue from a box on the coffee table and dabbed at her eyes.

"We only want information leading to the killer. We're not interested in anything else on the laptop," he assured her. "We'll return it as soon as possible."

She nodded, looking down at her hands. "Okay. I need to know who killed my husband. I can't stand the thought of someone out there enjoying their freedom after taking my husband's life," she said, relenting.

"We appreciate that," Ethan said as she got up and went to another room.

She was back within a few moments. "I just don't know what he could have gotten himself into," she said as she held the laptop out to Ethan.

"The sooner we get to the bottom of this, the better," Ethan said, taking the laptop from her.

"I appreciate that," she said.

"We're looking into who may have had keys to the haunted house," Ethan said. "Right now, it's just too early to give you any answers."

"When I was down at the gas station filling my car with gas, the girl that worked there told me there was a curse on this town. I told her there's no such thing as a curse," she said and chuckled bitterly. "But then she pointed out the other recent murders and the fire. And then I remembered that I heard about the curse when I was a girl. Back then, there had suddenly been a string of murders in Pumpkin Hollow, too. I know it sounds absurd, but it does make you wonder."

"Veronica," Ethan said. "I don't believe in curses. I do believe there have been some people who chose to handle their problems in a very inappropriate way and murdered some innocent people. But I do not believe in curses. We'll get to the bottom of who killed your husband. I promise you that."

My heart sank at the thought that the rumor of a curse was spreading all over town. It was mind-boggling. These people weren't just whispering about it or wondering if it might be true, but they were actually out there telling people it was true, and that concerned me.

"Officer Banks," Veronica said. "I want you to know something. I loved my husband with all my heart. We were married for thirty years, and I thought I would spend the rest of my life with him. Now he's gone, and no one knows a thing about what happened. I'm not threatening you, but I'm telling you right now that you and your police force need to find out who killed my husband and arrest them."

"Veronica, I assure you that we are doing everything we can to find your husband's killer. We need more time. But I assure you, we're going to find the killer."

I didn't look over at Ethan. I could tell by the tension in his voice that he didn't like what Veronica had just said.

"I'm sorry," she said, looking away. "It's just that my world has crashed in on me. I know you're doing everything you can, and I appreciate that more than words can say. Please forgive me if I sound rude."

"I understand completely," Ethan said, relaxing. "We'll find whoever killed your husband."

Ethan went over some questions with Veronica, but her answers didn't reveal anything new. No one seemed to know anything about the murder, and unless that laptop held some answers, this would be a difficult case to solve.

When we were back in the car, I turned to look at him. "What do you make of all this?"

"What I make of it is that we still don't have much of anything to go on. I had better figure something out soon, though. I'd hate for this to be my one and only case as a detective."

"What do you mean?"

"I'd hate to be fired because I couldn't find the killer on my first case."

Chapter Fourteen

"WE'RE FINALLY GOING to put an end to that silly Halloween season," Stella Moretti said. Stella owned the Sweet Goblin Bakery just down the street from the candy shop. You would have thought that a Halloween themed business owner would have been desperately trying to save the Halloween season, but several others owned Halloween businesses that were against it as well. It would have been better for all of us if they had just moved across town and operated as ordinary businesses, but they were all against doing that.

I rolled my eyes behind Stella's back. It wasn't very adult-like, but I was getting tired of hearing people badmouth the Halloween season.

"Come on, Mia," Ethan said. "Let's go inside."

Ethan was dressed in business casual today, and I couldn't help but think how sharp he looked. Ethan was going to be a great detective one day. We found a seat near the front of the room and waited.

Tracy Goode was filling in for our now-deceased mayor, Stan Goodall. Stan had come to an untimely demise a couple of weeks earlier.

I looked over at Ethan. "I wonder who's going to be our permanent mayor," I whispered.

"It's so close to being time to vote, I heard that Tracy will fill in for a while, and we will just vote like we normally would have if Stan hadn't died."

"That makes sense. Actually, it's one of the few things that does make sense around here anymore," I muttered.

Tracy sat down at the desk and called the meeting to order. I looked around me and was surprised that there weren't very many people here. I had expected a larger turnout, but I was glad to see that a lot of the business owners were here. Tracy read the minutes from the last meeting and then lay down the paper she held in her hand.

"At this point council members have decided that we will not vote on whether to end the Halloween season. We're going to table the measure for now."

There was a groan that went up from the people who wanted to end the Halloween season. I looked around me, and about a dozen people were shaking their heads and whispering.

"The city council has found that the original motion to end the Halloween season went against the bylaws of this town. In the future, if someone would like to put up a motion to end the Halloween season, it needs to go through the proper channels. If anybody wants details on what those channels are, they'll need to see the mayor, which is temporarily myself," Tracy continued.

I held my breath.

Stella jumped to her feet, moving faster than I had ever seen her move. "You can't do that! We're supposed to be allowed to vote!"

"Mrs. Moretti," Tracy said. "You're out of order. We have researched this, and we have found no cause to bring this motion to an open vote at this time. As I said earlier, if you want to file another motion, you'll have to abide by the laws."

Ethan and I looked at each other wide-eyed. "Did she just say what I think she said?" I asked him.

Ethan nodded. "She sure did."

I was stunned. I thought for sure we would have another fight on our hands. Ever since this measure was filed, it had been a source of worry for me. The Halloween season was so important to this town that I didn't know how we would function without it. There were a lot of business owners that relied on the Halloween season, including businesses not in the Halloween business district. We had several hotels and motels that might have gone out of business had there not been people coming to visit the town for the Halloween season, as well as restaurants and other shops.

I reached over and took Ethan's hand, and he squeezed my hand. I couldn't help but grin like a fool. We were going to be able to keep the Halloween season. At least for now. We sat and listened to everything else that came before the city council, hoping it would be a short meeting. Some people that had been in favor of ending the Halloween season got up and left while Tracy still spoke. I thought it was rude.

When the meeting ended, Ethan and I hurried outside. He pulled me to him, kissing me. "Like I said before, there's no curse on Pumpkin Hollow."

"I never doubted it for a minute," I said.

Fagan Branigan ran up to us, clapping Ethan on the back. "We did it! We are going to keep the Halloween season." Fagan owned the Little Shop of Costumes and had been on our side from the beginning.

Several other business owners gathered around us, and we all congratulated one another. I felt like a weight had been lifted from my shoulders. The Halloween season would remain.

"Mia, I think it was because you made the city website. I've had so many people mention that they saw us on the web, and they stopped in because of how lively and entertaining your website is," Polly Givens, owner of the Pumpkin Hollow Gift Shop, said.

"I just did what I thought might help everyone. It's because all of you have such wonderful businesses, and Pumpkin Hollow is such a wonderful town," I said, beaming.

I was excited beyond words. To think that we were finally going to end the stress of the motion to end the Halloween season made me giddy.

Chapter Fifteen

I HAD FILLED MY CAR with all my belongings and drove over to my new house. Parking in the driveway, I got out and just stood there looking at it. It was a cute little cottage painted white with black shutters, just like Ethan's house across the street. Everything had happened so fast—I had filled out the application one day, and the landlord had called first thing the next morning to give me the good news. Mom and Dad were surprised, and maybe a little sad that I was moving out. I had kept my move a secret from Ethan. I wanted it to be a surprise.

The key was in my pocket, and I pulled it out, heading to the front door. I was giddy as I stuck the key into the lock and turned it, pushing the door open. The scent of fresh paint still hung in the air, but I didn't mind. I walked into the house and stopped, looking around, and imagined all the possibilities. It had honey-colored hardwood floors and a lovely picture window in front. I would have to go shopping for furniture, but I didn't mind.

I dropped the duffle bag I was carrying onto the floor and brought the bag of cleaning supplies into the kitchen, setting it on the counter. The house was as clean as could be, but I still liked knowing it was up to my standards of cleanliness. I planned on spending most of the morning cleaning.

"I'm going to have to buy a lot of furniture," I murmured to myself.

I had left the front door open behind me, and when I turned around, a black cat was sitting in my doorway. "Well, hello, you," I said to the cat. "Who do you belong to? Are you the welcoming committee?"

I went to the cat, reached down, and scratched him between the ears. The cat looked up at me as if to say, *are you my new friend?* I scratched him under the chin and giggled.

"I guess you can hang around, but don't be surprised if I put you to work," I said and stepped past the cat, heading back to my car. I had filled up garbage bags with clothes, shoes, toiletries, and everything else I owned. My mother gave me a couple of small cardboard boxes that I filled with books and other odds and ends, but all in all, it was a small, sad lot for a twenty-eight-year-old woman.

I picked up four of the trash bags and headed back into the house with them, dropping them onto the living room floor. I needed bookshelves as well as living room furniture. I went to my purse and pulled out a small pad of paper and a pen and began making a list of all the things I would need. I didn't care that the house was empty, I was just excited that I had my own place again.

When I made another trip out to my car, I saw Ethan standing out in his yard watering his tree. He looked at me, did a double-take, and then smiled.

"Hey Mia, what are you doing over there?" he called from across the street.

I waved at him. "Just moving in. How are you this morning?" I glanced at my front door and saw that the cat had followed me out as far as the front steps and sat down to wait for me.

"Are you serious?" he asked.

"I'm as serious as I can be," I laughed. "I've just got a few more things to bring into the house, and I'm done moving."

Ethan turned the water off and then crossed the street. "Are you seriously moving in?" he asked again, grinning at me.

"I told you I was," I said with a laugh.

"Why didn't you tell me before now? Here, let me get that box for you," he said and reached for the box still in my trunk.

"Because I wasn't sure if I was going to get the house, and I wanted to surprise you. You don't mind me living this close to you, do you?" I asked and picked up the other box from the trunk.

"Are you kidding me? Why would I mind?"

He followed me into the house with the box, and the cat trailed behind us.

"You can just put that anywhere; I don't have any furniture yet."

"We'll have to get that situation fixed," he said. "At least these houses come with a stove and refrigerator so you don't have to buy those."

"I know, I'm so glad of that," I said as the cat rubbed up against my legs. I squatted down and ran my hand along the cat's back and up his tail. "Whose kitty is this?"

"I don't know who he belongs to," Ethan said. "I've seen him in the neighborhood for the past month or so, and I occasionally put some food out for him. I don't know if he has a home or not."

"I guess he's the welcoming committee then," I said and rubbed the cat's head. "I haven't had a cat since I was a girl. Maybe he'll hang out and keep me company."

I stood up and looked at Ethan. He still had a grin on his face, and we stood there like two silly people just standing and looking at each other.

"I'm glad you're moving in," he said after a minute. "It will be nice having you so close."

"I took your advice," I said. "I did what I felt like I needed to do and got my own place. Thanks for the encouragement, I've been feeling a little awkward since I moved back to Pumpkin Hollow. Those Masters degrees seem kind of useless right now, and living with my parents made it worse."

"I bet you'll get some use out of those degrees," he said. "It just takes time."

"I'm sure you're right. I guess I better get to the store. I need to get clothes hangers, laundry soap, and—oh, my gosh, I forgot. I don't have a washer and dryer. I guess I have to get one of each of those, too," I laughed.

"You can just cross the street and use mine, I don't mind at all," he said with a grin. "You're more than welcome to help yourself to anything that you need at my house."

"That's so sweet of you," I said. "I appreciate that."

I was sure I was going to enjoy living across the street from Ethan. I loved the neighborhood, and I loved this little house.

It was only one bedroom and one bath, and not very big at all, but it was perfect. Getting to decorate it the way I wanted to was going to be such fun.

Chapter Sixteen

I WAS IN THE KITCHEN at the candy shop mixing sugar and corn syrup together when there was a knock, and then the back door opened. I looked up from the mixer and was surprised to see Carrie Green standing there. She smiled big at me, her blond hair put up in a bun on top of her head.

"Hi Mia!" she said excitedly. "You'll never believe this, but your mother hired me without even needing to look at my resume. She remembered me from when we were in school, not that I expected that she wouldn't. But I came in here yesterday and bought some fudge, and she hired me on the spot. I still have to finish up a few more shifts at Pizza Town because I don't want to leave them in the lurch, but I get to work here!"

"Wow, Carrie," I said. "That's exciting news! Are you working a shift right now? I forgot to ask my mom how the interviewing was going, but I'm glad she hired you."

"I start on Monday. I just thought I would stop in and see how you were doing. I'm so excited about this opportunity, I know I'm going to enjoy this job so much more than Pizza

Town," she said and walked over and peered into the bowl I was adding ingredients to. "What are you making?"

"It's salt water taffy," I said. "I'm going to make some orange and black licorice-flavored taffy, but I'll make some other flavors, too."

"Will I get to make candy, too?" she asked. "My sweet tooth is going to get me in trouble around here."

"If you want to learn, we'll certainly teach you. Lisa has never made candy, she just helps out front. I'm sure Mom would be thrilled to have another candy maker on staff."

"I'd love to learn," she said, watching as the big silver mixer mixed the sugar and other ingredients together. "Hey Mia, I heard you and Ethan are a thing. Is it true?"

I couldn't stop myself from grinning. "Well, if you want to know the truth, I have to say it's true. I can hardly believe he's interested in me."

"Why would you say that?" she exclaimed. "You're a cute girl, and you've got a great personality."

I shrugged, looking at her. "I guess it's that old high school thing following me around. I mean it's not like I have low self-esteem or anything like that, it's just that I always considered Ethan, well, one of the popular kids."

"And I bet if you asked him about it, he wouldn't know what you were talking about. I got to know Ethan a few years ago when he dated my cousin. He's a very down-to-earth guy, and he's very easy going. I'm really glad you guys are together."

Carrie was right. Ethan was very down to earth and very sweet. It made me wonder if I had misjudged him all those years during junior high and high school.

"I'm sure you're right," I said. I weighed out some butter on the scale. Several years earlier I had tried to convince my mother to weigh the ingredients instead of measuring them. She had always done what my grandmother had done, and it worked great for her, but I needed to use the scales. My mother and grandmother seemed instinctively to understand when a recipe needed a little more of this or a little more of that. I just wasn't quite up to their candy-making skills, but I was working on it.

"Do you want to know something?" Carrie asked me.

I looked at her and nodded. "What?"

"I wouldn't bring this up, but you had asked me about Frank. Well, I have some news. Frank was caught stealing money out of the cash register at Pizza Town."

"Seriously? What happened?" I asked, turning to look at her.

"I told you about his family helping him to keep his job at Pizza Town, so it's not like they were going to call the police on him, but he had worked a shift, and his register came up short. He tried to blame it on someone else, but you have to put a code in before you ring a customer up. And only one person uses a register at a time, so we all know what happened."

"Has this happened before?" I asked, placing the butter into the bowl of the mixer.

"Not that I'm aware of," she said, leaning against the counter. "But it wouldn't surprise me if it had happened and his aunt kept it quiet. If you want to know the truth, I've often thought he was doing drugs. I mean, if you're only working two or three hours a day, you can't even afford to pay for rent. He lives with his mother some weeks, and then other weeks he stays with his aunt. I'm sure any money he gets goes to drugs or alcohol or whatever."

I stopped and considered what she was saying. Frank certainly seemed to have his issues, but what did that mean? Had he killed Greg? There was no way really to know at this point since we didn't even know why Greg was in the haunted house after hours. But it was something to think about and discuss with Ethan.

"Do you know how much money he took?" I asked.

She nodded. "I was closing that night, so when he turned up short, I helped him look for it. He made this big to-do about wondering how the money could have disappeared. He even searched underneath the counter like it could have slipped out of the drawer. That made no sense whatsoever to me, but I helped him count his drawer down. And he was short $322.12."

"Twelve cents?" I said. "That's weird, but maybe he did it to try to throw everyone off of thinking he stole the money?"

Carrie nodded. "That's exactly what I thought. For a minute I thought, how on earth could he have lost such an odd amount? But then I realized he probably did it on purpose because then he started claiming the register was computerized and that it had some sort of glitch. I'll tell you what, I'm glad to be getting out of there. It's hard to work in a place where one employee is not only favored but is covered for when he screws up or steals money."

"I don't blame you a bit," I said.

Things were getting stranger and stranger. I had a bad feeling about Frank. I didn't like him. And what Carrie had just told me confirmed to me that my suspicions about him were right. Something just wasn't right with him.

Chapter Seventeen

"HELLO THERE, MIA," a voice said from behind me.

Startled, I jumped up from where I'd been dusting the bottom shelves in the candy shop. I looked up to see Veronica Richardson. "Hello, Veronica," I said. "How are you doing?"

She gave me a sad smile. Her eyes were still puffy and red, and it broke my heart to see her that way. I couldn't imagine my husband being murdered and then getting a phone call by way of breaking the news.

"I guess I'm as good as I'm ever going to be," she said. "I don't know what to do with myself if you want to know the truth. I keep thinking of all the things I need to do for the funeral, but I don't want to do it. I guess maybe I feel like if I don't do any of it, maybe it will mean my husband's not really dead. Silly, I know." She gave me that sad smile again.

"I think I can kind of understand that. It's a hard thing to accept, and I certainly don't blame you for feeling the way you do."

"Thanks," she said softly. "I guess I'm just putting off the inevitable."

"I know it's small comfort, but I know the police are doing all they can to find your husband's killer," I said. "I wish you had been able to find something among his personal effects that would have helped."

"Actually, now that you bring that up, I did find something. I finally remembered Greg's email password, and I took a look at his email using my computer. There was very little email in there, but there *was* one from Charlie McGrath asking to meet with him," she said, looking at me pointedly.

I stared at her a few seconds before answering. "Did your husband respond?" I asked.

"If he did, he deleted it. It looked like he kept his inbox pretty well cleared out. There wasn't much from before the day he died."

"That's very interesting. Did Charlie say why he wanted to meet with him?" I asked.

She shook her head. "No. I'm on my way over to speak to Ethan now. Maybe his email password is the same one to get into the laptop."

"Wow. That could be the information the police have been looking for," I said thoughtfully. What if Charlie did know something about why Greg was in the haunted house that night? And what if he actually killed Greg?

"I think I'm going to have to try some of that pumpkin fudge," she said, pointing to the display case and changing the subject. "And then I'm going to head over and speak to Ethan Banks about what I found. The sooner they find my husband's killer, the better."

I went around to the other side of the counter and opened the back of the display case. "How much fudge would you like?"

"A quarter of a pound," she said. "I suppose Greg could have gone in there to enjoy the haunted house, and there was some derelict hanging around in there that took advantage of him and killed him. Or maybe Charlie had some sort of business to attend to with him, although I can't imagine what. Or maybe Charlie killed him." She chuckled bitterly and shook her head. "I just want my husband's killer found."

I cut a piece of fudge and took it to the scale, weighed it, and put it in a cute Halloween print paper bag. "Try not to jump to conclusions yet. Ethan will get to the bottom of all of this." I said it as kindly as I could. It was clear she was already suffering, and I didn't want her to get too invested in thinking it was Charlie if he hadn't murdered Greg.

I didn't want to speculate with her too much on who the murderer might be. I didn't want to bring any more trouble to Pumpkin Hollow, and I knew Ethan was doing his best to find the killer.

I wasn't completely sure that what she said made sense. A Friday night during Halloween season would mean plenty of guests in the haunted house. Then the house was searched before they locked it up. Although, at this point, I did somewhat doubt if any of Charlie's employees would have done a very thorough job of searching it. It seemed that things were done very loosely at the haunted house, and Charlie hadn't done much to correct that situation. He hadn't even checked to make sure that Gary had had new keys made. That meant that Greg might have stayed behind in the haunted house for some reason if he didn't meet the killer there after hours. I could understand that teenagers did that kind of thing, but not a grown man. And the email from Charlie was intriguing.

I rang up the fudge, and she paid with a debit card. "Thank you so much, Veronica," I said.

"Thank you, Mia," she said taking the bag from me. "Well, wish me luck. This is just one more thing that I need to do concerning my husband's death that will drive home the point that he's really gone. He isn't coming back." Her voice cracked on the last part, and tears sprang to her eyes. She nodded at me and turned around and walked out the door.

I watched her go, feeling bad for her. I hoped Charlie hadn't killed Greg, but I wanted whoever had done it to be caught as soon as possible. I just hoped Ethan could use the information contained in Greg's emails to find the killer.

Chapter Eighteen

AFTER WORK THAT EVENING, I went across the street to see Ethan. I loved having him living so close to me. I reached out to knock on his door and glanced at the ground near my feet. The black cat was sitting on the front step, looking at Ethan's front door expectantly. "What are you doing over here?" I asked him. He looked up at me and meowed. "Well, don't be disappointed if he doesn't let you in, and don't take it personally. He might be feeding you, but some people aren't cat people."

I knocked and waited for him to answer. When Ethan opened the door, I gave him a big smile and tipped my head toward the cat.

"Hey Mia, how are you doing?" he looked down at the cat. "And you brought a friend?"

"I'm doing fine. I hope you don't mind him coming along and making it a party," I said and stepped through the door as he held it open for me. "I've decided to name him Boo."

"A friend of yours is a friend of mine," he said. "Welcome, Boo."

"Wow, it's nice to come into a house where there's actual furniture to sit down on. You must be the upper class," I said, flopping down on his sofa.

He chuckled at me. "Some of us know how to live. What can I say?"

"I have something to tell you," I said. "My mom hired Carrie Green part-time, and she stopped in to say hello today. She had some interesting news."

"What did she have to say? And can I get you something to drink?"

"Water would be great. Carrie said Frank Garcia was caught stealing from the cash register at Pizza Town."

"Really?" he said over his shoulder as he headed to the kitchen.

"Really," I confirmed.

Ethan brought back a bottle of cold water, and handed it to me. "Did they file a police report?" he asked.

"No, not with his aunt being the assistant manager there. According to Carrie, she's always covering up for him. He stole over three hundred dollars from the cash register and tried to cover it up by saying there was a computer glitch that made the cash register report more money taken in than there actually was. Carrie thinks he's doing drugs. He lives for a few weeks at his mom's house and then a few weeks at his aunt's house and doesn't seem to take responsibility for anything."

He sat down on the sofa next to me. "Between you and me, we're trying to get an arrest warrant issued for him for vandalism. But it hasn't happened yet, so we need to keep it quiet."

I nodded and took a sip of my water. "I hope that happens. I think if he's desperate for money, maybe he lured Greg into the haunted house to rob him, things went wrong, and he ended up killing him."

"It's a possibility," he said, thinking it over. "Still, we don't have a lot of evidence for Frank being the killer."

"What about that broken window in the basement?" I asked.

"There weren't any fingerprints around the broken window. I thought someone might have tried opening it to get out of the haunted house, and when it wouldn't open, they broke it. But no fingerprints."

"It may still have happened that way. The window is at street level and faces the back of the house. Maybe the killer was wearing gloves."

Before he could respond, Boo jumped up on the sofa and started kneading Ethan's leg. "Make yourself at home, Boo."

"I think he just did," I said and ran my hand along Boo's back. "Veronica also dropped by the candy store today. I feel so bad for her, she's a nice person. Did she stop by to talk to you about the email she found?"

"She did. The password worked on the laptop, and we found some more emails from Charlie McGrath in a file. We're waiting on a judge to issue an arrest warrant," he said. "Again, we've got to keep it quiet."

I gasped. "Really? Charlie did it?"

"It looks that way. We should get the warrant before morning."

I sat back on the sofa. "Charlie McGrath. I don't know, Ethan. Something in my gut says otherwise. What was in the email that made you decide to get a warrant?"

"I can't tell you everything, but Charlie wanted to meet Greg at the haunted house the day Greg was killed."

I was having a hard time believing Charlie had done it. He just didn't seem like a killer, not that that meant anything. "Charlie did it," I said, thinking it over.

He nodded. "Greg wanted to buy the haunted house out from under Charlie, and Charlie got mad and killed him," Ethan said quietly. "It's the only thing that makes sense."

"That does make sense," I said thoughtfully. "I just don't feel right about it. But what about Frank?"

"He was definitely there at the haunted house that night, but we're not sure how he fits in with the murder. Maybe Charlie will enlighten us when we arrest him," he said.

I nodded. "Charlie and Frank? I can't imagine them in on the murder together, but I guess crazier things have happened."

"You can say that again," Ethan said.

I was troubled about Charlie being arrested for the murder, and I wasn't sure why. Maybe it was because I liked Charlie and didn't want to think of him as a killer. Or maybe I was overlooking something.

I was able to see Frank as the killer, though.

Chapter Nineteen

THE FOLLOWING DAY I baked up a batch of orange cupcakes and topped them with chocolate frosting. On the tops of them, I piped white frosting ghosts. While I worked, I went over everything we knew about Greg's murder in my mind. Unless Charlie really did lure him into the haunted house, it made no sense that he was in there at all. I sighed. Somebody somewhere had to know what happened, and they were keeping that information to themselves. I put the cupcakes in the display case on the shelf beneath the fudge. Fudge was one of our best sellers and was always front and center on the top shelf of the display case.

The cupcakes had been selling well since we had introduced them several weeks earlier, and I was surprised we hadn't had any trouble with Stella Moretti about selling baked goods. I expected it would only be a matter of time before she came in and had a fit over it. But Stella only halfway participated in baking and selling Halloween-themed goods in her bakery. She hated the Halloween season. The problem was, she was the

Halloween themed bakery, and the city council kept a tight hold on what businesses did in the Halloween business district.

"I think the cupcakes were a good idea," Mom said, coming in from the kitchen. She carried a tray of orange lollipops that she had drawn black cats onto with sugar.

"Those turned out so cute," I said, looking at the tray of lollipops. "And I do think the cupcakes were a great idea. If Stella decides she doesn't want to participate in the Halloween season, then we will just pick up the slack where we can."

"Speaking of the Halloween season," she said and set the tray of lollipops on the front counter. "I'm so glad we got the good news that we will be continuing it."

"Me too, it's the best news we've had in over a month. I'm really concerned about the trouble we've been having lately. But our luck has got to change soon, doesn't it?"

"I agree with you one-hundred percent," she said. "We'll just stay positive."

"If you don't mind, Mom, I think I'm going to take some cupcakes down to Ethan and the other officers to thank them for all the hard work they do for this community."

"That sounds like a great idea. You go ahead. I think I'm done making candy for the morning. We're pretty well filled up with everything now," she said as she arranged the orange lollipops in a cute fall-themed tin. She had wrapped each lollipop in clear cellophane and tied them with either orange or black sateen ribbons.

"I'll be back in just a few minutes then," I said and headed back to the kitchen to get the rest of the cupcakes I had made. I put them in a carrier and headed out the door.

"I BROUGHT TREATS FOR the hardest working police officers in the state," I said to Ethan as I held the cupcake carrier out to him.

"Oh wow, Mia, that was so nice of you to think of us," he said and took the carrier from me, leaned over, and gave me a quick kiss.

We were standing in the break room at the police station. There was half a box of donuts on the table, and I pushed them over a little so Ethan could set the box of cupcakes down. Opening the lid, I could smell the wonderful aroma of orange and chocolate.

"Those look good," Ethan said as he reached for one. "By the way, we got the arrest warrant, and a couple of officers have gone to pick up Charlie."

I looked at him. "Really? I was kind of hoping the judge would say there wasn't enough evidence."

"What? You don't want me to be successful on my first case and put away the killer?" he asked, cocking one eyebrow and tilting his head toward me.

"Of course I want you to be successful on your first case. I was just hoping it wouldn't be Charlie," I assured him. "If you think there's enough evidence to convict him, then I'm glad a killer will be off the streets."

He held the cupcake to his nose and inhaled. "Well, if you do the crime, you gotta do the time. You know what they say," he said with a grin. "This smells so great." He began peeling the cupcake liner away from the cupcake when we heard loud voices coming down the hall.

"What's going on?" I asked, turning toward the open door.

Ethan set his cupcake down on the table and headed to the door. "I'll take a quick look," he said over his shoulder.

I followed Ethan to the door and watched as Charlie was brought down the hallway in handcuffs by two officers. He was quiet, with his head hung low, but his wife was hot on their heels.

"You can't do this! You have no right! I'm going to get a lawyer!" she cried, following behind the officers.

"Ma'am, you need to keep your distance," Officer Ramirez warned her.

"Don't tell me what to do! You have no right to do this. You have no proof!" she cried.

Ethan hurried to Evelyn, holding his hands up to her. "Evelyn, let's try to calm down. We have an arrest warrant to bring Charlie in. You're not making things any easier."

"I don't care what you have. This is a mistake! You'll be hearing from my lawyer, I already called him!" Evelyn's curly hair hung limply above her shoulders, and her cheeks glowed red. The anger that rolled off her was frightening.

"We will be happy to speak with your lawyer," Ethan said calmly. "We're just doing our jobs, Evelyn."

The officers steered Charlie into the receiving area and closed the door behind them.

"Ethan Banks, this is a terrible mistake," Evelyn said, putting her hands on her hips. "I want to speak to the chief. Now. Someone is going to pay for this. No one arrests my husband without cause and gets away with it." She narrowed her eyes at Ethan and jutted her chin out.

"The chief is out of the office on business right now. If you want to go to the reception area, you can wait there, and as soon as he returns, I'm sure he will speak to you," Ethan told her firmly. "But you cannot stay here if you aren't going to keep your voice down."

Evelyn huffed at Ethan and opened her mouth to say something else when she caught sight of me standing in the doorway. She turned and looked at me. "Mia, tell him what a mistake this is. You know Charlie. He could never kill anyone. He couldn't hurt a fly, and you know as well as I do that this is a terrible mistake."

I wished I had stayed back in the break room where she couldn't see me. There wasn't anything I could do to help Charlie at this point, as much as I wished he wasn't in this predicament. "I'm so sorry, Evelyn," I said. I didn't know what else to say to her. "I'm sure your lawyer will sort this thing out. I'm so sorry."

She strode toward me taking long steps and stopped in front of me. "This is a sad day in Pumpkin Hollow when somebody as decent and upstanding as my husband has been arrested for a crime he did not commit. I'm going to speak to my lawyer all right, and we will get to the bottom of this. I don't know who killed Greg Richardson, but it wasn't my husband." She turned and headed back toward the door she had come in, shoving it open with her open palms.

After the door closed behind her, Ethan turned to look at me. "I wish things hadn't turned out the way they did, either. It really is kind of a sad day for Pumpkin Hollow, isn't it?"

I nodded. "But maybe there's been a mistake. Maybe you'll come up with more evidence, and it'll be somebody else that killed Greg."

He nodded. "I think I need a cupcake now. Stress makes me want sugar." He gave me a grin and walked past me and back to his cupcake.

I did hope that Charlie didn't kill Greg Richardson. Part of me wished there would be some other explanation like some stranger had killed him, but in my heart, I knew that that wasn't the truth, either.

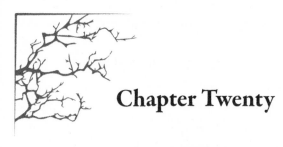

Chapter Twenty

THE FOLLOWING DAYS were quiet ones for Pumpkin Hollow. Charlie was arrested for Greg's murder, and Greg's funeral had taken place earlier in the week. I considered going to the funeral, but I wasn't close to either Greg or his wife, and I thought it might be an intrusion. Funerals were a personal occasion to be shared by family and close friends.

I was hanging Halloween decorations in my new house, and Boo was rubbing up against my legs as I used a thumbtack to hang a vintage black cat Halloween cutout on the wall of my living room by a black ribbon. I had been collecting vintage Halloween decorations for years, and I had a lot of really cute items.

"Boo, I think this looks just like you." The vintage paperboard cutout looked back at me with its yellow eyes and seemed to grin. No one had claimed Boo, and I had begun to think of him as mine.

There was a knock at the door, and I left my decorating to see who it was. Ethan stood on my front step when I opened the door. "Well, hello there," I greeted him. I pushed the door open wider for him to enter.

He gave me a quick kiss. "Hello Mia, and Boo," he said and bent over to scratch Boo's head.

"You'll spoil him if you give him what he wants every time you see him," I warned and headed back into the living room.

"I guess it's a risk I'm willing to take," he said with a chuckle. "Looks like you're making things festive in here."

"I needed something to put me in a good mood, and Halloween always puts me in a good mood."

"I don't know if you heard or not, but I've got news that might be of interest to you."

I looked at him. "Oh?"

He nodded and picked up a paperboard cut out of a big orange jack-o'-lantern with a small black cat laying across the top of it. "We arrested Frank Garcia today."

"Really? For Greg's murder?" It wouldn't surprise me if Frank had committed Greg's murder, but I wanted to know if Charlie was released. "What about Charlie?"

"No, Frank was arrested for graffiti in the haunted house. We checked down at the hardware store, and the day before Greg was killed, Frank had bought two cans each of green and black spray paint. We had also checked the security camera at the haunted house. The camera was extremely outdated, but there was a very blurry, spotty image of someone that looked like Frank. We needed more evidence to arrest him, so we held onto that until we found out about the spray paint he bought. His fingerprints were all over the place in the haunted house, which isn't surprising considering he worked there, but we've got enough to convict him on vandalism."

"Okay," I said, thinking this over. "Now you have proof that he was in the haunted house the night that Greg was killed. So why isn't he being charged with his murder? And is the murder on the videotape?"

"The video camera was in the lobby of the haunted house. And unfortunately, that's the only video camera in the entire haunted house. If Charlie had invested in decent cameras, the camera probably would have caught the killer and maybe set him free if it really wasn't him. But as it is, there was only one camera. Frank finally admitted he still had a key, and he also admitted to spray-painting the haunted house. He let himself in the front door, and that's why he was on the camera. However, our killer most likely entered through another door since no one else came through the front door that night."

"The killer entered through another door, not the broken window?" I asked.

"Just like we suspected, that window was broken to make it appear as if someone had broken in. But we know that didn't happen."

"And why don't you think Frank killed Greg?" I asked, still holding out hope that it was him. "Maybe Greg was already in the haunted house when Frank got there. He could have come in during business hours and hid until everyone left."

"We've got a time stamp on the camera. It didn't take Frank long to spray graffiti on the wall, and he would have needed additional time to kill Greg. He just didn't have enough time. Besides, why would Greg stay in there after closing?"

I sat down on the sofa, and Boo immediately jumped in my lap. I ran my hand along his back and gently scratched the base of his tail. "So you got Frank to admit he was in the haunted house that night, and that he left the graffiti on the wall. I assume it's because he was afraid he was going to be charged with murder?"

Ethan sat down next to me and ran his hand over Boo's head. "That's exactly what happened. Frank's afraid he's going to have a murder pinned on him, so he confessed to the graffiti."

"And are you sure the murder shouldn't be pinned on him?"

"Everything points to Charlie. We still have a lot of work to do though, and Charlie is still maintaining his innocence."

"Have you been in touch with his lawyer?" I asked.

He nodded and chuckled. "Oh yes, we've been in touch with his lawyer. But the chief still feels Charlie is our man."

"Well, I guess for now that's the way things are. But I really think Frank is the murderer. We already know he and his aunt lied about him being at work that night. He isn't going to tell the truth about it."

"I went down and had a talk with his aunt without Frank around. She was very nervous and admitted that she didn't remember whether Frank was at work or not. I asked about timecards, and then she had to admit he frequently forges timecards, and they just pay him whatever he writes down."

I sighed. "Well, this is something," I said. "At least Frank will be charged with vandalism. I just hope if Charlie is innocent that he will get off."

He nodded. "At this point, it doesn't look good for Charlie."

All I wanted was for the killer to be put away. I was tired of thinking about the case.

Chapter Twenty-One

"WHAT ARE YOU SO DOWN about?" Carrie asked me when I finished ringing up a customer. It was just after ten o'clock, and I had been clock-watching all morning.

I glanced over at her. I was glad we had hired her; Mom had told me how much work she had been doing around the shop since she had started working there a week earlier. She also had a lot of great ideas for new flavors of different candies.

I shrugged. "I don't know, I guess I'm just feeling a little down about the fact that it was Charlie McGrath that murdered Greg. I really had it in my mind that it was Frank Garcia. I thought he was the one."

"To tell you the truth, I kind of felt the same way. I never liked him. And I'm glad I don't have to work with him anymore," she said and snitched a gumdrop out of the bulk bin. "Your mom is going to have to weigh me at the beginning of my shift and then at the end of my shift and charge me for all I've eaten during the day. I'm afraid I'm probably putting away a lot of candy."

"I think she figures in a certain amount of employee bonus candy when she figures out how much she needs each day," I said with a chuckle. "I'm going to have to get on the treadmill myself if I don't stop snitching candy."

"How does Ethan like his new position?" she asked, straightening jars of candy on the front counter.

"He likes it a lot. He's a little bummed that he's still on patrol most of the time, but I think once he takes the test to become a detective, that will give him some leverage for a real promotion."

Mom came out of the kitchen carrying a tray of yellow, orange, and chocolate mounds of candy on it. "Guess what I did?" she sang out.

"What are those?" I asked, eyeing the baking tray she held. Each mound was about the size and shape of an egg split in half crosswise.

"I was experimenting with meringue, and I made these sweet little bundles of lovely goodness. They're kind of a mix between meringue and marshmallow. I flavored each one differently. Chocolate, orange, and banana."

Each mound had a spider web drawn on in thin dark chocolate, and in the center of each spider web was a little milk chocolate brown spider with googly eyes drawn on. "Those are so cute!" I said.

"Oh, my goodness, those look good," Carrie said. "I'm going to have to hit the treadmill with you, Mia, if I expect to not gain any weight from working here. Those are darling!"

"Well, don't just stand there and stare. I want you both to taste test them," Mom said, holding the tray out toward us.

"You don't have to tell me twice," I said and reached for an orange one. Carrie picked up a chocolate one, and we both took a bite. I groaned in pleasure. They were light and airy, and yet very marshmallowy in the center. The flavor was exactly right. Not too sweet or overpowering, but still enough flavor to let you really taste it. "These are delicious, Mom. I don't know how you do it."

"Perfection," Carrie said and took another bite.

"You girls are good for my ego," Mom said with a laugh and made some room in the display case for the new candy.

The front door swung open, and Ethan walked in with a grin. "I think this is my favorite place in town. Every time I open that door, the smell of chocolate and sweet goodness hits me." He walked up to the counter and peered over the side, looking at the tray Mom held in her hands.

"Ethan, you need to try out the new candy I made. I'm still working on a name for them, but the girls have decided that they taste okay."

Ethan grinned at her and reached for a chocolate one. "I bet they said they were more than okay," he said.

"You know we did," I told him. "These are wonderful."

He took a bite and smiled. "Wonderful is the right word," he agreed. "These are great."

"So Ethan," Mom said as she put the remainder of the candies into the display case. "Mia said Charlie McGrath killed Greg Richardson. I have to say, I'm surprised by that."

He nodded. "I think a lot of people are surprised by that," he said. "Of course, he maintains his innocence. But as far as

I'm concerned, my job is just about done there. He has a good lawyer, and I'm sure he'll get a fair trial."

"Still, I kind of wish it was somebody else," I said. "I mean, it doesn't really matter, I guess. Greg is dead, and nothing is bringing him back. It's sad no matter who the killer is."

He nodded. "I enjoy figuring out who did what in a case, but I don't like to see our friends or neighbors arrested and maybe spending the rest of their lives in jail."

I nodded my agreement. "So Ethan," I said, leaning on the counter. "Boo says he misses you and he'd like to invite you to dinner tonight."

"Boo?" Mom asked looking at me. "Who is Boo?"

"Oh, I guess I forgot to tell you. When I moved into my new house, there was a sweet little black cat that was hanging around. He just invited himself into my home and into my life. So now, I'm a cat owner."

"Oh, I see," she said, nodding. "I think Millie misses you. Maybe you could bring her over to meet Boo?"

Millie was our former neighbor's dog. I thought Mom and Dad were probably far too attached to her for me to take her with me, and so I had left Millie with them knowing I would get to see her regularly. "We might have to do that sometime."

"Well," Ethan said after swallowing the bite of candy he had in his mouth. "I hate to disappoint Boo. He seems like someone you don't want to disappoint. I'll be off work at seven if that's not too late."

"Seven o'clock is perfect," I said to him.

I planned on making tacos, and I would need to stop by the grocery store and pick up some cheese before I went home. That would give me plenty of time between when I got off work at six and when Ethan would be home from work after seven.

Chapter Twenty-Two

"HELLO EVELYN," I SAID as Evelyn McGrath approached the front counter at the candy store. I hadn't expected to see her here so soon after Charlie's arrest. I noticed the dark circles under her eyes.

She gave me a forced smile. "I suppose you've heard, no wait, you were there at the police station, weren't you? I'm so sorry, I feel so frazzled these days. I don't know if I'm coming or going." She held a coffee cup from Brian and Amanda's coffee shop in one hand and her purse in the other.

"That's completely understandable," I said. "I'm so sorry about what happened." I didn't know what else to say to her. What do you tell a woman when her husband has been arrested for murder? Whether he did it or not, I knew that she was suffering.

"Thank you," she said, and her eyes went to the display case. "I asked Ethan if I could bring Charlie some fudge. He loves your mother's peanut butter fudge. Ethan said it would be okay, so I thought I'd stop in before you closed." Her eyes came back to me, and I could see the unshed tears in them.

I nodded. "Let me get that for you. How much would you like?"

"A quarter of a pound," she said. "I don't suppose he has a way to store more than that. So maybe I'll just come back every night for the next few days and bring him some fudge." She smiled, but her voice cracked.

"I'm sorry Evelyn, if there's anything I can do for you, don't hesitate to ask," I said as I cut a piece of peanut butter fudge for her.

"That's very kind of you, Mia," she said. "I need the support of my community now more than ever. But don't think this means I'm giving up. We've got a good lawyer, and I just know he's going to make sure the truth is known about Charlie. He didn't kill anyone. It's crazy to think he would ever harm anyone. He's the kindest, sweetest man I know. He's been under such strain lately because we've been having some financial struggles. Oh, I'm sorry, Mia," she said. "You don't want to hear all this." She chuckled and waved her hand as if she could wave away her troubles.

"Evelyn, if you ever need to talk, I'm here. You can tell me anything, and I'll keep it between the two of us." It was out of my mouth before I thought it through. It might not have been the best thing to say. I couldn't keep things from Ethan. And she might say something he needed to know about the case.

"I appreciate that more than you know," she said, nodding her head. A tear slipped out of one eye, and she wiped it away with her finger. "Oh Mia, here I am holding onto this empty coffee cup." She laughed. "I probably drank the contents of it more than an hour ago. Can you throw this away for me?"

"I sure can," I said and reached for the coffee cup. There was a small trashcan that I had been getting ready to empty back behind the counter, and I tossed the cup on the top of everything else that was in it.

I cut and wrapped the fudge, put it in a bag, and handed it to her. "This is on the house. You tell Charlie I'm thinking of him."

Evelyn's eyes lit up. "That's so sweet of you, Mia. Thank you. Well, I better get going if I'm going to drop this off this evening. But first I need to stop by the house and pick him up a couple of his spy novels. He loves to read, thank goodness he'll have something to do while in that horrible jail. But like I said earlier, this is temporary. I just keep telling myself that, and I know it's the truth."

"You're welcome, Evelyn," I said. "Remember, if you need anything else you just let me know."

"Thank you so much, Mia," she said and headed toward the door. "You're a lifesaver!" And then she was gone.

It was nearly six o'clock and almost closing time for a weeknight at the candy shop. On weekends we stayed open until nine o'clock during the Halloween season for the tourists that were visiting the different attractions in town.

The front door swung open, and my friend Amanda walked in with a smile on her face. "Hey Mia, I'm so glad I caught you guys before you closed. I've had fudge on the brain for days now, and I keep meaning to stop in. I've been so busy down at the coffee shop, and by the time I remember, you guys are closed."

"Well, I'm glad you made it in. We're all out of pumpkin spice fudge, but we've got plenty of vanilla, chocolate walnut, peanut butter, and candy corn left."

"I think I'm going to have to try a quarter pound of the candy corn, and maybe a quarter pound of the vanilla. And while I'm here, I think Brian would love some of those candy corn marshmallows. What are these cute little candies with little spiders painted on them?" she asked, peering in at the candy my mother had made earlier.

"My mom made those earlier today, and we haven't come up with a name for them yet. So if you think of something cute, you let me know. They're really good, and I think you'll love them."

"I'll have to think on a name for them," she said with a chuckle. "Why don't you give me one of each flavor?"

"You got it," I said and began cutting the fudge.

"Mia, did you hear what happened with Charlie McGrath? I can hardly believe he killed Greg Richardson," she said, looking at me wide-eyed. "I just saw Evelyn leaving here. Poor thing."

"I know, it makes me sad. I thought Charlie was a really good guy, and it makes me sad for Evelyn, not to mention Pumpkin Hollow. We didn't need another murder." I still wasn't sure he had done it, but Ethan was convinced.

"I was just talking to Brian about it today. Evelyn came into the coffee shop the morning Greg was killed, and since we weren't busy yet, we talked for a few minutes about the Halloween season. The poor woman. I'm sure she had no idea what was going on with her husband. Along with the money problems they've been having, I think it must be a tremendous strain on her. It seemed like she was kind of shaky as we talked that morning."

I looked up at her and stopped in the middle of wrapping her candy corn fudge. "She stopped by the coffee shop the morning Greg was killed?" My eyes went to the coffee cup I had thrown away for Evelyn just a few minutes earlier. There was bright pink lipstick on the lid.

She nodded. "Yes, I remember it was Saturday because when I heard about the murder, I immediately thought about Evelyn and our conversation about the haunted house having financial difficulties. I thought how terrible it was that now there was a murder at the haunted house. It's heartbreaking."

"Can you remember what time of morning it was?" I asked her and continued wrapping her fudge.

"First thing. When I went to unlock the door, she was waiting out front. Why?"

The coffee shop opened at six a.m. I had intended to ask Amanda if anyone unusual had come into the coffee shop that morning, but I had forgotten. "I was just wondering," I said and looked over at Lisa. "Lisa? Can you come over and finish putting Amanda's order together?"

"Sure," Lisa said and came over to where I stood. I glanced down at the coffee cup in the trashcan and picked it up. Then I looked up at Amanda. "I'm sorry, Amanda, I'm going to have to let Lisa finish up with you here. I'll get back with you in the next day or two, and we can catch up on things, okay?"

Amanda looked at me with her eyebrows furrowed. "Sure, Mia, no problem. Is everything okay?"

"Everything is fine," I said and grabbed my purse from under the front counter, and headed for the door. "Lisa, tell my mom that I left a little early and let her know I'll get ahold of her later. And please don't forget to clean up and lock up the shop when you're done."

I got into my car and stopped for a moment to call Ethan. I placed the coffee cup in the cup holder in my car and waited for him to answer the phone. When there was no answer, I hit end and started my car.

Chapter Twenty-Three

EVELYN HAD ONLY LEFT the candy shop a few minutes earlier. She had mentioned stopping by her house to get novels for Charlie, so I headed over to the police station to see if she had made it there yet. I drove through the police station parking lot and didn't see her red SUV. I hesitated before leaving the parking lot, looking for Ethan's pickup. His vehicle wasn't there either, so I left and drove by Ethan's house to see if he had gotten off work early.

There were no vehicles in front of Ethan's house, so I decided to drive past Evelyn's house and see if she was there. It might have been wiser to go back to the police station and wait there for her, but the adrenaline was rushing through my body, and I needed to do something.

When I turned down Evelyn's street, I slowed down. Her red SUV was parked in the driveway of her house, and I drove slowly past it, trying to decide what to do.

When I got to the end of the block, I made a U-turn and drove back by, slowing down again when I was in front of her house. I couldn't see any movement through the sheer curtains on the windows at the front of the house, so I drove to the other end of the block. I made another U-turn and came back. I slowed my car down again and realized that I just needed to get out of there and go back to the police station and find Ethan. He needed to know what was going on because we had the wrong person in jail for Greg's murder. But as I started to put my foot on the gas, Evelyn emerged from her house. When she saw me, she stopped in her tracks. She looked at me quizzically and then smiled.

Before I had time to think I pulled my car over and got out. My body was shaking with adrenaline as I walked toward her. She had several paperbacks in one hand along with the bag of fudge I had given her and what looked like a man's sweater over her arm.

"Mia, I didn't expect to see you so soon. What are you up to?" she asked as she closed the distance between us.

My eyes went to the books in her hand. "You're on your way to the jail now?" I asked.

She nodded. "Yes, I told you I needed to stop by the house and pick up some paperbacks for Charlie. I also thought I'd bring him a sweater; he gets chilly, and I don't know what the temperature is like in that jail cell. I hate to even think about him being there at all if you want to know the truth. It just makes me sick to my stomach."

I nodded. "I would imagine it's cold in there. Not that I really know, of course."

"Mia, is there something I can do for you?" she asked, scrutinizing me as I stood there.

"Charlie is innocent, isn't he?" I asked her.

She nodded and then narrowed her eyes at me. "Yes, Mia, he really is innocent."

"I thought so. I didn't feel right about it when he was arrested. I thought it was Frank Garcia, but Ethan and the other officers thought it was Charlie. But something about that just didn't sit right in my gut."

She looked at me somberly. "Your gut instincts are correct. There's no way my Charlie could have killed Greg. He couldn't have killed anyone. He just doesn't have the heart for that sort of thing."

"Do you?" I asked. "Do you have the heart for that sort of thing?"

She moved two steps closer to me, and I stepped back one. "It all depends. If someone were trying to hurt someone that I love, I think I could find it in me to do that. But not Charlie. Bless his heart, I know he loves me more than anything in this whole world. But I'm afraid he couldn't kill someone to protect me. I can tell you one thing though, no one is going to hurt my Charlie. I would do whatever I had to do to protect him."

I nodded. "I think I can understand that. But was Charlie ever really in any kind of mortal danger?"

"Let's just say, he may not have been in any present mortal danger, but someone wanted to take something very dear from him. It was the thing that he had worked all of his life for, and he loved it almost as much as he loved me. It was breaking his heart, someone wanting to take that from him."

"I can understand that fear can take over a person's life, and you feeling that you had to do something drastic. But what I can't understand is murder." I stood and stared at her, waiting to see what she would do next. Every nerve in my body was standing on end, and I wondered if anyone was home in the nearby houses, and could I count on them should things get out of hand?

Her mouth made a hard line. "You just don't understand. You haven't spent your life with someone you love more than life itself. Until something like that happens, I don't think you're in a place to judge."

"I guess you can say I'm judging," I said. "But didn't Greg have a right to live his life with the person he had loved all his life?"

She tilted her chin upward in consideration of my words. "Maybe. But I guess you can say I'm just like a mama bear. Don't come near the ones I love, or else."

"So I guess that's an admission of guilt? What did Greg do that was so terrible?"

"He tried to take the haunted house away from Charlie. I had no choice in the matter, I had to do what needed to be done. Poor Charlie had worried himself nearly to death, and I was scared he would have a stroke or heart attack. He was up all night pacing the floor. The doctor told him his blood pressure was out of control, and if he didn't do something soon, it would be the death of him. So you see Mia, my Charlie's life was at stake. He had worn a hole through his stomach with worry, and the doctor said his heart would be next."

I nodded, the phone in my hand was at my side. "Are you going to let Charlie go to prison for what you did?"

She shook her head. "No. I told you, I have the best lawyer money can buy. He's actually my cousin, and he owes me a favor. And besides that, there's no evidence that Charlie did anything because he didn't do it. I'm confident he'll get off. The problem I find myself with now is that you figured this out. And I'm certainly not going to jail for murder."

Before I knew what was happening, she drew a gun from her purse with her free hand and held it on me.

"Evelyn, you don't want to do this. We don't have to go there," I said, trying to remain calm.

"I'm afraid you backed me into a corner, Mia. Get into my car," she said, motioning to her red SUV with the gun.

My mind scrambled for a way out. I was not getting in that car, and I was not going anywhere with her. Nor was she going to get away with Greg's murder. But I was stuck right then, and I very hesitantly turned toward her car. At that moment, she closed the short distance between us and pointed the gun at my ribs. Before I had time to think, I drew back my elbow and hit her in the chest with it. She screamed and lost control of the gun as it flew out of her hand. I kicked back at her shin, and she went down on one knee while I scrambled for the gun.

Grabbing the gun, I pointed it at her. My hands shook, and my head pounded, and I told myself not to pull the trigger accidentally.

"I'm sorry, Evelyn, but you're not getting away with Greg's murder."

Evelyn turned to me and through gritted teeth said, "I am not going to jail. Do you hear me? I had no choice but to kill the person that was killing my husband. It was practically self-defense. There was nothing else I could do, don't you see that?"

"Evelyn, you can tell yourself anything you want, and you can even feel justified in your actions, but the rest of the world will see your actions as inexcusable."

While keeping the gun trained on her, I dialed 911.

Chapter Twenty-Four

BOO PURRED LOUDLY AND rubbed up against Ethan's leg. After a moment he jumped onto Ethan's lap, demanding to be pet.

"You're kind of bossy, aren't you?" Ethan said to Boo. He was answered with loud purring.

"I'd say Boo is pretty fond of you," I said as I sat next to Ethan on my brand new sofa. I had ordered a sofa and loveseat two days earlier, and it had been delivered late in the afternoon. We had had to skip dinner the night before when the police had arrived and arrested Evelyn at her home, and I had to go down to the station and give my statement. Thankfully, Ethan was at the station by the time I arrived, and he took my statement from me. The adrenaline had been coursing through my body so hard I was shaking as I told him what happened.

"I'm glad you put things together and recognized the lipstick on Evelyn's coffee cup," Ethan said with a chuckle.

"If you want to know the truth, I kind of surprised myself. I mean, there were times that I wondered about Evelyn, obviously.

And of course, I didn't feel that Charlie was the killer, but I still would have put my money on Frank. That is, until Amanda mentioned Evelyn buying coffee from her shop early in the morning on the day Greg was killed. I would never have put it together if Evelyn hadn't just come in and handed me that coffee cup with the same shade of hot pink lipstick on the lid."

"Yeah well, it was pretty good detective work. I might have to take some tips from you," he said and scratched Boo's head. "I'll never understand criminals that think they're justified in their actions."

"Me either," I said and ran my hand across Boo's shoulders. "I get it that Charlie and Evelyn had financial troubles, and I get it that financial problems are extremely stressful. Some people don't handle stress very well at all, and I guess that was Charlie. But it seems like there had to be another way out of this thing other than killing Greg."

"It's a shame, really," Ethan said. "Everybody's a loser here. Sure, maybe Charlie will be able to figure a way to save the haunted house, but Greg lost his life, and Evelyn lost her freedom, so in effect, Charlie also lost his wife. And still, for now, the financial troubles remain."

"Did she say how it all went down?" I asked him.

"She did. Knowing the haunted house was in foreclosure, Greg had made Charlie an offer. Evelyn said it was ridiculously low, and she wouldn't let Charlie accept it. She said Greg kept hounding Charlie about accepting his offer, telling him he could get out from under the financial burden of the haunted house, and if he didn't accept it, the bank would take the haunted house, and he would end up with nothing. Charlie was under a great deal of stress over it all and was making himself sick."

"Evelyn mentioned it was making him sick," I said and scratched Boo's ear.

He nodded. "Evelyn got tired of what she called Greg's harassment of Charlie and decided to put an end to it by creating a fake email account in Charlie's name. She emailed Greg and told him to meet her at the haunted house and had him enter by the back door which is why he never showed up on the camera near the front door."

"And she killed him with the spear? Just like that?" I asked him. "Wasn't Greg suspicious when she showed up at the haunted house and not Charlie?"

"She told him Charlie had gotten sick that morning and asked her to show up in his stead. She let him into the haunted house under the ruse that they needed a higher offer from Greg. She showed him around, pointing out how much the haunted house was worth until they got to the caveman display. There she stabbed him with the spear. But things didn't go as planned," he said.

"What do you mean?" I asked. "He's dead, and that's what she wanted, right?"

"She did get the intended end result, but not in the way she wanted. She was surprised to see the graffiti and was worried someone was in the haunted house with them, but when she didn't see anyone, she continued with her plan. Except her plan was to make it look like that plastic caveman mannequin had fallen on Greg and he was accidentally stabbed by its spear."

"Seriously?" I asked. "She wanted to blame it on the mannequin?"

"She thought she could arrange it to look like an accident and get away with it. But the mannequin was a much lighter weight than she had anticipated, and she couldn't get the thing to lay down on top of Greg at the correct angle."

I turned toward him. Ethan was trying to suppress a smile. "That's nuts. That thing wasn't flexible, and there was no way it could have landed at the right angle."

"No, it wasn't flexible at all. It was poor planning, to be sure."

"It sounded like a lot worse than poor planning," I said.

"Later she hoped that whoever had gotten into the haunted house to spray the graffiti would be blamed for the murder. That's why she kept trying to point at others. She just couldn't come up with a very good reason for Greg to be in the haunted house after hours."

"What a heck of a time for Frank to choose to vandalize the haunted house."

"Yeah, that was crazy, wasn't it?"

"Wait, did Charlie know she had killed Greg? When he got to the haunted house, he looked kind of frazzled."

"No, he didn't know. But he did know Evelyn had left the house early in the morning, and she insisted he tell me that they were both at home. So, I'm sure he suspected something, but Evelyn insists he never asked her if she killed Greg."

I nodded and sighed. "I hope this is the end of the troubles for Pumpkin Hollow. On the bright side, we're keeping the

Halloween season, but I don't know if it will matter if we lose any more attractions."

"I guess that just means we're going to have to work harder to make up the difference," Ethan said. "I still think that the goat-tying event might be a real possibility."

I chuckled. "Do you know someplace we can round up a bunch of goats really quick?"

"I guess that might be a problem," he said. "But maybe I'll make a couple of phone calls. Do you remember Tom Baker from high school?"

"The name sounds familiar. Remind me."

"He was on the football team and played halfback," he said. "Remember? Red hair and kind of stocky?"

I nodded. "I do think I remember him. He was kind of quiet, wasn't he?"

"Yes, he was quiet. And it just so happens that his dad owns a farm down the road aways. Maybe he's got some goats we can borrow."

"Oh?" I said, thinking this over. "And maybe he's got some extra bales of straw that we could use for people to sit on and watch the goat tying?"

"It wouldn't surprise me one bit if he did," he said. "I'll make a phone call tomorrow, but I can't promise anything."

"You don't have to promise anything. I've got some other ideas to fill in the gaps, too. I just hope we can pull it together quickly."

I looked at Ethan as he rubbed Boo's head. Ethan was a good guy, in spite of the rough start we had had back in the seventh grade. I hoped he would be in my life for quite a while to come.

The End

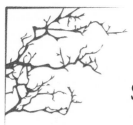

Sneak Peek

DEATH AND SWEETS

A Pumpkin Hollow Mystery

Chapter One

"Mia, get it together," I muttered to myself, shaking my head.

I yawned as I drove down the street toward the Sweet Goblin Bakery. I wasn't normally up and out the door at five a.m., but my mother had called me at four a.m. and asked me to go into the candy shop early to start making the candy for her. She didn't feel well and didn't know if she would be in at all, but she said she hoped to be in later. I usually went to work at nine and hadn't expected the early morning call, so I was still groggy with sleep and trying to keep my eyes open. A stop by the donut shop would help me get going with a donut or two and a big cup of coffee.

It was early October, and the air was crisp and cold. Stars still twinkled in the early morning sky, and the moon was still out. I had donned a warm, fuzzy red sweater, jeans, and my brown suede boots that came up mid-calf. My hair was tucked beneath a white knit hat, a few strands of my brown hair peeked out from beneath it.

Pumpkin Hollow is a small town in Northern California that celebrates Halloween all year long. We had an assortment of tourist attractions, and we saw a lot of business during what we called the Halloween season. The Halloween season ran from Labor Day weekend until about two weeks after Halloween, and we were in the thick of the season now.

Things were finally going well for me, now that I had moved back to Pumpkin Hollow after being away for ten years. I had a new boyfriend, a very cute and sweet Officer Ethan Banks, my own house—it was rented—and a new pet, my little black kitty named Boo. In spite of all the trouble we had had in Pumpkin Hollow this Halloween season, I was still reasonably happy with my life and the way things were going.

When I pulled up to the bakery, I noticed the lights were still off. I glanced at the clock on my dashboard. It read 5:13 a.m. That was unusual. Stella Moretti owned the Sweet Goblin Bakery, and she was normally very punctual in opening each day. She did a brisk business early in the morning with people stopping in to pick up donuts and coffee before heading out to their jobs.

The Pumpkin Hollow Candy Store was only a couple of blocks away, but I parked in front of the bakery since I had to pass it to get to the candy shop. I got out of my car, headed to the front of the bakery, and peered in through the window, but I didn't see any movement. That was odd.

I glanced at the front door and noticed that it was slightly ajar. Maybe Stella had gotten busy in the back room making donuts and forgot to come out front to turn the lights on, I thought.

I gently pushed open the door and stepped inside the bakery. I couldn't smell baking donuts or cupcakes, and I didn't know what to make of that.

"Stella?" I called out to the darkness. Silence greeted me. It wasn't like Stella not to be here early, busily baking up a storm for her customers.

"Stella?" I called louder. When there was still no answer, I felt the hair on the back of my neck stand up. It was cold inside the bakery, and I wondered why Stella hadn't turned on the heater. I went to the front counter and peered over at the cash register. Had she been robbed? The drawer was closed, so I thought that wasn't likely.

I pulled my cell phone out of my front pocket, just in case, and strained my ears to hear. I was met with deafening silence, as a feeling of dread came over me. I glanced down at my cell phone, and it showed the time was 5:15.

"Stella?" I called out, sounding more hopeful than I felt. Maybe she was running behind this morning and hadn't gotten her baking started. I took a few more steps toward the back room where the kitchen was. There was a light switch on the wall on this side of the kitchen doorway, and I flipped it on. The front of the bakery flooded with light behind me.

"Stella?" I called again, more quietly this time.

Something inside of me said to turn and run, but my feet were glued to the spot. I squinted my eyes into the darkness of the kitchen. I could make out the kitchen island where Stella decorated cookies, cupcakes, donuts, and cakes. The oven sat cold in its corner, and the industrial-sized refrigerator suddenly came to life. I jumped and then realized the refrigerator compressor had kicked on. Where could Stella be? I swallowed hard and took two steps into the kitchen.

I knew it was pointless to call out again, but I couldn't help myself. "Stella?" I said in my normal tone of voice.

I reached back and ran my hand along the wall on the inside of the kitchen doorway and felt the light switch. I swallowed again and flipped the switch on. The kitchen was flooded with light, and I had to shield my eyes from the brightness for a moment.

When my eyes adjusted, I remove my hand and glanced around the kitchen. What I saw gave me goosebumps. There was flour on the kitchen countertops, dirty mixing bowls, and the big stainless steel stand mixer had batter dripping down the outside of the bowl. This was completely unlike Stella. She would never leave her kitchen in a mess after a workday, and this mess was clearly left from the previous night.

Stella had been a difficult person to deal with when the city council had tried to cancel the Halloween season. She sided with the city council. But Stella knew how to conduct her business, and a dirty kitchen was not something she would tolerate.

I slowly walked farther into the kitchen, my boot heels clicking and echoing on the kitchen's tile floor. I surveyed the mess and wondered what to do. I didn't know Stella well enough to have her home phone number. Had she had an emergency and needed to leave suddenly the night before? Maybe that was it. Maybe her husband had fallen ill, and she needed to leave without having a chance to clean up. Maybe she had made an emergency trip to the hospital over in the next town and had been up all night with him and hadn't made it in to clean up and open the bakery on time.

I thought this was a logical explanation. I decided that if I at least ran some hot water into the dirty bowls, it would help loosen the dried on batter, and it would give Stella a helping hand when she arrived later. I stuck my phone in my front pocket. Part of my brain said I was really reaching and making up a story here, but I picked up two dirty bowls from the counter and headed to the kitchen sink anyway. I set them in the sink and turned the water on, squirting dish soap into them, and watched them fill with hot water.

When the two bowls were full, I turned the water off and turned back to the kitchen island to get more dishes to put into the sink, and that was when my eyes landed on a pair of athletic shoes. There were feet and legs still in those shoes, and I realized somebody was lying behind the kitchen island. I took in a shaky breath.

"Stella?" I whispered, thinking she must have had a heart attack or some other medical emergency. I hurried to her side, kneeled down, and touched her shoulder. She was cold and stiff. "Stella," I whispered again.

I gently pushed on her shoulder, rolling her on her back, and her head turned toward me. I suppressed a scream and sat back on my heels. Her mouth was open, and her eyes stared vacantly. My eyes went to the red stain on the white apron she wore, and I jumped to my feet. Backing up quickly, my mind tried to grasp what I was seeing. When I got several feet away from her, I stopped and stared at her for a few moments. I pulled my phone from my pocket again and dialed Ethan.

"Ethan, I'm down here at the Sweet Goblin Bakery, and Stella Moretti is dead."

"What? Say that again?" he mumbled sleepily.

"Stella Moretti is dead. She's here in her bakery," I repeated. "Ethan, she's dead. There's blood on her apron, I need you to come down here. Now."

"I'll be right there," he said, sounding alert now. "I'll call for an ambulance and a squad car, and I'll be there in just a few minutes." He ended the call, and I stood with my cell phone still pressed to my ear and looked at Stella again.

What happened, Stella?

I shook myself, stuck my phone in my pocket, and headed out of the kitchen to pace back and forth in the bakery dining area. What had happened to poor Stella? What was going on here in Pumpkin Hollow?

I breathed out, trying to steady my nerves. Pumpkin Hollow had had a string of bad luck the last couple of months, and it seemed like the nightmare would never end. I went to the big picture window and looked up at the still-dark sky and willed Ethan to come faster.

Buy Death and Sweets at Amazon

https://www.amazon.com/gp/product/B07GN1S6HG

If you'd like updates on the newest books I'm writing, follow me on Amazon and Facebook:

https://www.facebook.com/
Kathleen-Suzette-Kate-Bell-authors-759206390932120/

https://www.amazon.com/Kathleen-Suzette/e/
B07B7D2S4W